Mind Bending Chronicles

Volume One

By T.C. Walker

ISBN 978-1-7351761-3-0

Published by T.C. Walker
Cover image by NASA

Table of Contents

Introduction

In Mind Bending Chronicles: Volume One, T.C. Walker brings you three mind bending stories of the strange and unusual.

In *Monkey*, you will meet a man imbued with the power of tremendous luck at gambling. Is it a gift or a curse? Perhaps both? Watch how he navigates the pitfalls of being able to conjure immense wealth at the drop of a hat!

Voices takes us into deep space, where NASA has lost contact with a survey ship orbiting Mars. A rescue mission is sent to investigate, and many interesting discoveries are made along the way... What secrets does the Solar System hold for humanity?

Finally, in *Operator*, we meet a brave American soldier who wakes up in cold, snowy, suburbia after being knocked unconscious from a roadside bomb in Iraq. Will he be able to untangle the mystery of why he is a stranger in his own life?

Your world will never be the same once you return from a trip through Mind Bending Chronicles: Volume One!

Monkey

Chapter One

Jack Cross sat in his car in the parking lot of Motley Rivers, LLC, a fledgling hedge fund operation, staring blankly at the plain brick wall in front of him. His boss had just laid him off, supposedly due to corporate downsizing and a somewhat dodgy economy, but Jack suspected there was more to it than that. On his way out the door, Cliff Bell, the Vice President in charge of Jack's division, handed him an envelope, claiming it contained a severance bonus.

"Now, Jack," Bell said, "it would be in everyone's best interest if you kept this under the table. Know what I mean?" Bell then shifted his gaze to a burly security guard standing nearby before extending his hand towards Jack.

Jack shook it and said, "Sure, whatever," before being escorted out of the building.

Down in the parking lot, Jack removed the envelope from his inner jacket pocket, assuming it contained at most maybe a grand or two, considering that was the usual bonus amount doled out by his bosses at various times throughout the year.

He was shocked to discover that the envelope contained a crisp stack of sequential $100 bills, with a paper band wrapped around it labeled $10,000. It was at this point Jack knew something was up with Motley Rivers, but ultimately, he didn't care. He was low enough on the totem pole that if anything illegal was going on, he had no idea what it was. Furthermore, Jack wasn't very sociable, and tended to shy away from office gossip and all of the "corporate culture" bullshit, so his coworkers in general didn't talk to him much and just let him do his job in peace.

Jack liked it that way. What he didn't like was being fired just days before his 53rd birthday, and mere months after his wife tragically passed away from cancer. Also within the last couple of years, his elderly dog had to be put down. Now he was sitting in his car with an envelope stuffed with what was most certainly ill-gotten gains that Motley Rivers was now frantically trying to offload for some reason. So far Jack Cross wasn't a big fan of what being in his 50's had to offer.

Out of the corner of his eye Jack saw the same burly security guard from upstairs approaching his driver's side window. Jack stuffed the envelope and money back into his jacket while rolling down the window. The guard put his hands on the door window sill and leaned in, almost uncomfortably close. So close, in fact, that Jack caught a hefty whiff of cologne and sweat from the guard's beefy neck. Jack could see that a name tag on the guard's shirt read "M. Deavers."

Deavers spoke in a raspy but gentle voice, "Mr. Cross, you're gonna have to go ahead and leave." He turned his head to look towards the office building, and then back to Jack, before lowering his voice, "Look, Mr. Cross… you seem like a good dude. I have some friends down at the precinct, and, well… If I were you, I'd take that envelope and get out of town for a couple weeks."

Deavers quickly stood up, rapped his knuckles on the roof of the car, and loudly bellowed, "Move along, sir. Thanks," before heading back in towards the building. Jack suspected that last bit was for show, in case anyone from the executive offices was listening or watching to make sure the guard was doing his job.

So, something *was* going on… something definitely illegal, if the police were going to be making a move in the next few weeks. Jack started his car as he rolled up the window and drove out of the parking lot.

For a few minutes, Jack worried that the $10,000 in his pocket was counterfeit. It was all so crisp and clean; it just looked so fake. He suddenly remembered that a junk drawer in his house contained one of those counterfeit detecting pens. Jack had bought it years ago for no real reason other than thinking it would be a cool thing to have on hand. He checked a few twenties and even a fifty once over the years just for fun, but since he mostly used credit cards for his purchases, the pen usually just sat idle in the junk drawer. It would now be the pen's time to shine…

Jack then wondered what he should actually *do* with the money. He and his wife had paid off their house years ago, he had a healthy emergency fund, his retirement accounts were well above those of most other people his age, he paid his credit cards off every month, and he had no other debts. Jack was a frugal person and a simple man with very few expenses.

He could simply sock the money away into a bank or retirement account, but then he remembered what Cliff Bell had told him about keeping the money "under the table." Depositing all ten grand at once into a bank would generate a transaction report. Although not indicative of anything illegal, it might raise some flags with the police if they start investigating Motley Rivers and their employees. Breaking up the money and depositing it in chunks, however, *was* illegal,

Jack knew, and was referred to as "structuring." He certainly wouldn't be doing that.

Ten thousand dollars was a nice chunk of money, but not so much that it was hard to hold on to or spend in small doses every once in a while. Jack decided his best course of action was to just keep the money in the small safe in his home office, and dip into it every once in a while to buy groceries or a nice bottle of cognac.

On the short but boring drive home, Jack then began fantasizing about having much more than $10,000 in ill-gotten cash, and how he might have to launder it. He had a movie fan's knowledge of money laundering, and he was sure that was a dumbed-down and probably dangerously inaccurate vision.

Jack remembered a news story he had read years ago about a man finding a paper bag containing $250,000 in cash along the railroad tracks. He immediately turned it in to the police, and when a news reporter asked him if he considered just keeping the money and not telling anyone, he replied, "Lady, I have a jar of change on my dresser that's been there since the '70's. I wouldn't even know what to do with that much hard cash."

Jack pulled into his driveway shortly after 4pm. He had been fired prior to his usual quitting time of 5pm, so now he had an extra hour at the end the day to sit on his couch feeling sorry for himself.

No, he thought… I'm not gonna do that. I just need to think things out logically…

After checking the mailbox (empty), Jack unlocked his front door and walked directly to his home office. He tossed the envelope of cash down next to the keyboard of his computer before removing his suit jacket and kicking off his shoes.

While his computer booted up, Jack fixed himself an ice-cold Cuba Libre and took a few sips while staring out of the kitchen window and pondering the day's events. Snapping back to life, he went to his office, sat at his desk, logged in to his bank accounts and retirement accounts, and opened a spreadsheet detailing his personal finances. Jack crunched a few numbers, ran a few retirement calculations, and, after finishing his drink, immediately starting feeling better about having been fired.

In theory, Jack never had to save another penny for retirement. He had enough money in his IRA and 401k that even with moderate stock market returns, he would be sitting on almost $1.5 million by the time he turned 62. Throw Social Security on top of that, and he was already set up for a decent retirement.

The more pressing issue was providing for his current living requirements. Finding another job at 53 was far easier said than done, but Jack had some leeway. He was generally financially conservative by nature, so he had almost $35,000 in bonds and cash accounts designated as "rainy day" or emergency funding. This amount was enough to pay Jack's bills for a good two years, maybe even two-and-a-half if he moderately adjusted his standard of living.

These calculations were all made even before accounting for the $10,000 in cash sitting next to the keyboard. This would easily cover a good six or seven months of bills and food if needed. It was at this point Jack remembered what the security guard had told him about getting out of town for a couple of weeks. He wondered if the guard meant that Jack should just treat himself to a nice vacation, or if he should literally leave town because something bad might happen otherwise.

Jack checked some plane ticket prices online for several destinations, and wow, were they expensive for last-minute, even for someone with ten grand to burn. He figured if he was going anywhere on vacation this late

9

in the game, he should probably drive. But not just yet. Jack had generally liked his job, as well as the people he worked with, but for the first time since being fired a couple of hours earlier, he felt free and optimistic about the future. He wasn't exactly sure why; maybe it was the rum, or, all things considered, his extremely stable financial situation. He had lost so much over the last few years, and after sitting down and actually thinking things out logically, he was finally starting to get tired of feeling sad and numb about his life.

Jack wanted to celebrate.

Chapter Two

After a quick shower, Jack dressed in jeans, a white t-shirt, and an olive drab windbreaker. He peeled off three crisp hundred-dollar bills from the $10,000 stack, and, after verifying their authenticity with the counterfeit pen retrieved from his junk drawer, stuffed them into his front pocket. He locked the remaining cash in his top desk drawer and hid the key in its usual place behind a book on his bookshelf.

It was 6 o'clock on a Tuesday evening. Not exactly party time, but seeing as how Jack had nowhere to be for the foreseeable future, it was as good a time as any to cut loose and have a little fun. He locked his front door, hopped in his car, and headed downtown to one of the several Tribal casinos in the city.

Jack was normally not a fan of the stricter rules and more limited gaming of the Tribal casinos; Vegas was more his style, and he headed out there at least once a year. However, he was playing with "house money," Motley Rivers' money, before even setting foot in the door, so he figured he could make an exception just this once.

Parking directly under a streetlight in the immense parking lot of the casino, Jack made note of the huge number "8" painted on a sign bolted to the post. He walked inside the casino and immediately to the nearest bar, where he ordered a glass of champagne. Hey, let's party, he said to himself. Jack dropped a $5 bill in the bartender's tip jar after he graciously broke one of the hundred-dollar bills for him, and then he headed to the gaming tables.

Jack decided to try his luck at Roulette. He bought in for $100, and the croupier pushed five stacks of 20 red plastic chips, valued at $1 apiece, over in front of him. There were three other people at the table; a nicely-dressed Asian couple who looked to be in their 40's, and a gruff-looking white woman on the wrong side of 60 dressed in jeans and a tank-top sporting a picture of a wolf howling at the moon. The white woman and the Asian man were both smoking cigarettes. Smoking was probably the one thing Jack loathed the most about casinos, but the air circulation in them was fairly state-of-the-art nowadays, so it didn't bother him too much.

The minimum bet at this Roulette table was $10, Inside or Outside. This meant that Jack had to either bet a total of $10 on at least one of the 38 red and black numbers on the layout (the "Inside"), or a total of $10 on at least one of the other bets (the "Outside" of the layout). The Outside bets included such options as Red, Black, Even, Odd, and various groupings of numbers. Jack decided to play the Inside, so he grabbed a stack of ten of his red chips and spread them out across ten different numbers. He chose 4, 5, 7, 8, 10, 12, 14, 20, 27, and 00. These numbers represented his birthday, his late wife's birthday, and several other "lucky" numbers.

The Asian couple was working with three stacks of green chips, and spread a good 20-25 of them across the Inside numbers. The other woman at the table seemed to be betting mostly on the Outside, and she placed a stack of five orange chips on Black, and five orange chips on Odd. At this point the small Roulette ball was quickly spinning around the slowly rotating wheel, and the croupier waved her hand across the layout, indicating no more bets could be placed. After a few more tense seconds, the ball began spiraling down towards the pockets of the Roulette wheel, and shortly thereafter began tink-tink-tinking its way in and out of the various numbered slots before coming to rest on the number 4.

"Yessss," Jack hissed. The croupier placed a clear plastic marker, similar to a large chess piece, on the layout space containing the number 4. The Asian couple had also put a chip there, so they congratulated each other.

The woman stubbed out her cigarette and said, "Well, at least I broke even." The number 4 was Black in Roulette, so the woman won $5 on her Black bet, but lost $5 on her Odd bet. The croupier swept away all of the losing chips before paying everyone out.

After winning 35 chips, but losing nine (for the numbers that didn't hit), Jack had cleared 26 chips, or $26, on his very first bet of the evening. The Asian couple had won about $10 on the spin, and they began talking to each other about what their strategy should be on the next spin. After everyone had collected their winnings, the next round of betting had begun.

Jack decided to test his luck, so he bet the same ten numbers again. The Asian couple pressed their winnings, and bet a good 30 or so chips across a smaller selection of numbers; maybe eight numbers, with two to four green chips each. The solo woman was almost out of chips when Jack walked up to the table, so she pushed her last 12 or so orange chips onto Black while rasping, "This'll have to be my last bet."

The croupier spun the ball and, after a few moments, waved her hand across the layout. The ball slowed, and made its way down the well before landing on 5. Jack had won again… another 35 chips, but losing 9. He was up another $26. The number 5 was red, so the woman lost her last 12 chips. The Asian couple had coincidentally bet with Jack again, so their three-chip bet on 5 yielded them $105. Their net gain on this coup was about $80, so they whooped and hollered and high-fived each other. They saw Jack smiling and high-fived him as well.

The woman left the table, leaving Jack and the Asian couple to themselves. Five more spins went by, and Jack continued to bet the same numbers. One of his numbers hit every single time. He hadn't lost in seven spins, ever since he first sat down. He was up almost $200, net. The Asian couple had won some and lost some, and Jack estimated that, since he had sat down, they were up by maybe the same amount as he was.

For a few brief seconds, Jack locked eyes with a man in a suit standing at a podium behind the gaming tables. He suddenly felt a tinge of paranoia, and decided he should change up his bets. He didn't want anybody to think he was doing something fishy, so he selected a completely different set of ten numbers. He did so randomly, just dropping down chip after chip across the layout, not even paying attention to the specific number.

All eyes were now on the ball, which came down on 32. Jack's eyes darted to the layout, where he saw a lone red chip sitting on 32. Another $26 in his pocket. Jack switched up his numbers again. Again, one of his selections hit, and the croupier pushed more winnings his way. The table had since run out of plain red chips to give Jack, so they had been paying him in regularly denominated casino chips for the last several wins. At this point the Asian couple decided to cash out, but Jack was not alone. There were three or four other people standing near the table and watching; passersby who noticed that Jack had not lost a single coup in almost ten spins.

Jack was getting nervous. The man in the suit walked up directly behind the croupier, and started watching the game intensely. For some reason he felt like he should lose some of his money back to the casino, so he did something he normally would have considered incredibly stupid and dropped a stack of twenty red chips on the number 0. Before the croupier could spin the ball back to life, one of the rubberneckers behind Jack stepped up to the table.

"Hold on a second," a portly fellow in a white button-down shirt said. He dug into his shirt pocket and fished out some casino chips.

The man, about Jack's age, spoke with a thick drawl: "I ain't seen you lose yet. I think you know somethin' I don't." He dropped a $25 chip on 0, right next to Jack's stack, and three other $25 chips on several other numbers.

By now there were about six or seven people watching the action at the Roulette table. The ball was spun, and, in what felt like no time flat, dropped down into the slot marked 0. Jack felt queasy, and his hands went numb. He suddenly got very hot, and the fat Southerner "woo"-ed and clapped Jack roughly on the back. Several of the spectators applauded behind Jack, and the croupier paid him $700 in chips.

Jack had won almost $1000 on a $100 buy-in, never losing once in ten spins of the wheel. He was attracting the wrong kind of attention, both from curious spectators and several men in suits working for the casino. Not for the money he had won; $1000 is peanuts in the grand scheme of things for a casino, but the fact that he had won so much is such a short amount of time betting straight up on single numbers was incredibly unlikely.

Jack really wanted to lose now, mostly as a show of good faith to the casino that he wasn't doing anything illegal. He placed twenty chips each on six consecutive

17

numbers; 16 through 21, the six numbers closest to him on the layout. He also placed another twenty chips on Black, and twenty on Even. Jack had $160 on the line. The crowd behind him attracted several more spectators, and two more people had bought in to the game and waited for Jack to bet before placing their chips right alongside his.

The croupier flicked the ball into the wheel, and everyone around the table went silent. Jack's armpits began dripping sweat, and the fat Southerner was rhythmically pounding the edge of the table with his fists. The Roulette ball dropped and landed squarely on number 20. The small crowd around the table cheered, and the Southerner's cry of joy hurt Jack's ears. Jack won $20 for betting on Black, $20 for Even, and another $700 for hitting 20. Minus the $100 for the other numbers he had bet on and missed, the croupier ended up paying Jack another $640.

By now one of the men in suits was on the phone, no doubt talking to someone in the surveillance department. They were probably backtracking every move Jack had made since entering the casino, wondering how someone could hit a number eleven times in a row right off the bat. Jack could feel his heart beating, and his mouth felt like it was full of cotton. He realized he had finished his champagne a while ago, and he desperately needed something else to drink.

"I'd like to color up, please," Jack said as he pushed his stack of chips to the croupier. The Southerner was talking to him, as were several other people, but he wasn't really hearing them. He just wanted to get his money and get away from that table. Something just felt wrong. The croupier ended up handing him three $500 chips and a few random other denominations. Jack stood up, stuffed the chips in his pocket, and headed to the bar.

Jack ended up sitting at the bar for close to an hour, mindlessly staring at the baseball game playing on one of the TVs mounted above the liquor shelves. After drinking a whiskey, neat, and nearing the end of a rather large margarita, Jack had finally started to cool down and relax for the first time since stepping in the casino.

He had replayed the events in his mind over and over again, and ultimately concluded that he had simply gotten incredibly lucky. After all, he had heard stories of Craps players rolling the dice for hours on end without Seven-ing out, so 11 wins in a row on a Roulette wheel was probably nothing. No security guards or men in suits had approached him or even seemed to be keeping an eye on him, so he figured they probably concluded the same as well.

Still, in all of his trips to Vegas, nothing like that had ever remotely happened to him, and he had certainly never won that much money in such a short amount of time. Now, he had almost $2000 in cash and chips in his pocket, a good buzz going, and the night was still young. He paid his bar tab, plucked another hundred-dollar bill out of his pocket, and headed towards the slots.

Jack found a somewhat secluded corner of the slot machine section, and sat down at a $1 machine featuring images of bikini clad women in seductive poses. He fed the hundred-dollar bill into the machine, which subsequently registered 100 credits for him to play with. He pressed a button to bet the minimum; one credit, or $1. Another button press set the digital wheels of the slot machine's computer screen spinning.

Jack looked away for a second to ogle a passing cocktail waitress, but a loud rhythmic wailing sound immediately drew his attention back to the slot machine. Jack looked at the screen, which was now filled with dollar signs and large-breasted cartoon women dancing erotically. He had just won $5,000.

"Fucking hell…"

Chapter Three

Jack left the casino almost $7000 richer than when he went in. After his slot machine win, some more casino suits appeared and tried to appear intimidating. By this point Jack was numb from the evening's events, so their sweat-job was having little effect on him. They lightened up, and even displayed sympathy, when he told them the story of how he had been fired earlier that day, and after filling out some paperwork they cashed out his chips, cut him a check, and he was on his way home.

Unable to sleep, Jack stayed up until almost 4am watching television and nursing some more alcohol. Tomorrow, he told himself, he would have to make sure to drink plenty of water, and maybe get in a good workout, too. Being laid off was no excuse to let one's health go to pot.

Jack slept on the couch that night in his clothes, and woke up the next day at about 10am. Wanting to make sure the previous night's events were not a dream, he checked the zippered pocket of his green windbreaker, and found a check for $5,000 and almost $2,000 in cash. He put the check and cash in the locked drawer of his desk before taking a shower and eating breakfast.

Jack thought about what to do with the $5,000. He couldn't just sit on a check like he could the cash; it was either take it to the bank or rip it up, and he certainly wasn't going to rip it up. He also didn't want to deposit it or cash it right away, since that might look suspicious if the police started investigating Motley Rivers and questioning ex-employees.

Although Jack had won the money fair and square and could easily prove it came from the casino, he still did not want to attract even the slightest bit of attention from anyone doing any kind of investigation. The casino's check had a generous 120-day expiration date, so he decided to just keep it locked up for a couple of months or so until any heat involving Motley Rivers had died down.

Aside from the check, Jack now had almost $12,000 in cash that he didn't have 24 hours ago, and, in Jack's personal financial mindset, it was all "off the books." He could flush that money completely down the toilet and still be in good shape, financially speaking. He decided to take the security guard's advice from the day before and immediately started packing his bags for a long trip out of town.

Jack's neighbor was a divorced, 66-year-old retired Army Colonel named Art

Hacker whose idea of Heaven was drinking beer, grilling hamburgers, and watching football all day. Despite those vices, he was also in amazing shape; after a lifetime of military service, he continued his fitness journey in retirement, and, every single day, he either lifted weights or ran countless laps around a nearby public track.

Hacker had often kept an eye on Jack's house whenever he was out of town, even going so far as to mow his lawn if needed. The pair had bonded almost immediately when Jack told him of his own brief stint in the Army and deployment to the Middle East. Jack informed Hacker of his job loss and how he would be taking a vacation for an undetermined amount of time, possibly up to two weeks. Hacker already had a set of Jack's house keys, and Jack slipped him a 24-pack of beer as thanks.

Jack had his car packed up and was on the road by early afternoon. He had considered a trip to Florida, but then changed his mind and decided to head West instead. He had some friends in Los Angeles he hadn't seen in years, and he also wanted to spend several days in Las Vegas. On the way out of town, Jack stopped at a gas station to fuel up and grab some snacks for the road. At the checkout counter, he spotted the small display

23

of lottery tickets, and told the cashier he wanted one $1 scratch-off ticket. This one was themed with cartoon dogs, and the grand prize was $4,000.

Jack had been formulating a theory since last night after leaving the casino. Every bet he placed had won. He had either gotten incredibly lucky over the course of a couple of hours, or he was somehow imbued with magical powers making it impossible for him to lose at gambling. He wanted to test his luck-slash-magical powers in a different venue. Sitting in the parking lot of the gas station, his hands trembling, he started scratching off the little windows of the lottery ticket with his car key. When he was finished, five golden chihuahuas stared up at him from the ticket. It was a winner. Four thousand dollars.

"Jesus Christ," Jack muttered to himself, and he tossed the ticket into the glove box of his car, almost as if it was burning his fingers. His net worth had grown by over $20,000 in less than two days, and it was all basically free money, acquired by him for doing absolutely nothing. He started the car and got back on the road.

Jack was almost certain now that some cosmic being was either screwing with him or generously bestowing wealth upon him for some unknown reason. Sure, he had had a rough couple of years, but nothing that had happened to him hadn't already happened to millions of people before him, and even worse things were happening to people now. Plus, he was pretty financially stable... he didn't *really* need the money, unless he couldn't find a job in the next 2-3 years. So why was he being gifted with this power?

Maybe this was some kind of cosmic test. Maybe he was supposed to be giving the money away, or spending it on something specific. He made a mental vow to himself then and there that as soon as he was able to cash in the lottery ticket, he would donate the entire $4,000 to charity, just in case, as some sort of goodwill gesture to the universe.

On the other hand, maybe this was some kind of curse. He saw the way the casino suits (as well as a couple of questionable-looking people standing behind him at the Roulette table) were eyeballing him as soon as he started winning. The whole ordeal made him feel physically ill. Sooner or later, if he kept gambling, and kept winning, it would attract too much attention, the kind of attention that gets people killed.

Jack had plenty of time to think about all of this on the road to Vegas. More pressingly, however, he had to decide what his plan of action would be once he actually got to Sin City. He couldn't just sit down at a Roulette table and immediately start winning every single coup. He would have suits and security guards all over him in less than 45 minutes.

If these gambling "powers" were real, he would need a much more subtle and judicious way of exploiting them. He briefly considered just buying a Powerball ticket, winning a billion dollars, and swearing off gambling for life, but that would be too high profile. Maybe just buy a bunch of million-dollar tickets? No, no, that would be way too suspicious. And, again, he thought, it's probably best not to win too much money at once. Even just winning $700 at once in Roulette made him feel uneasy, and drew too much attention.

He would need a plan to simply win small amounts of money, over and over again, all while avoiding suspicion. If he could do this and rack up, say, $2 million at *most* over the next couple of years, he would be set for life, and no one would be the wiser.

That is, assuming his powers would last that long. For all he knew, they dried up as soon as he bought that winning ticket at the gas station. Was there a time limit to these powers? Or maybe it was a monetary limit?

Maybe he was only "allowed" to win $20,000, or some other random amount. What if these powers were dangerous, and every time he used them, some horrible cancer was growing in his body? Or some random child in Africa dropped dead with every dollar won?

Jack had to snap himself out of it... he couldn't assume anything, good or bad, just yet. He had to think logically, and work with the information he was given. He had already won over $10,000 with these powers, and if he never won another penny, that's still a pretty good win.

Shortly after crossing the border into New Mexico, Jack began seeing signs for a casino in Albuquerque. Already having decided to stop in the city for the night, he figured he might as well stay at the casino's hotel and run a few more tests, albeit very discreet ones.

This casino was another Tribally owned property, and for a brief moment Jack felt guilty about knowingly using his magical powers to take money from Native Americans, but then decided to eventually donate some of the gas station lottery ticket money to a Native American cause. Yes, Jack would use his powers for good, as well as profiting a little for himself.

Being Wednesday night, the hotel was not crowded, and Jack had no problem getting a room. After freshening up a little and doing some stretches in his room, Jack locked the balance of his $12,000 in cash in the hotel room safe, and hit the casino floor with two $20 bills.

Jack walked up to an empty Blackjack table, said hello to the dealer, and dropped a twenty on the table. The dealer took it and gave Jack four $5 chips. The minimum bet on this table was $10, so Jack placed two of the chips on the betting circle closest to him. The dealer dealt the cards, and Jack drew a Blackjack. The dealer paid Jack $12 while making a comment about his being lucky "right off the bat," and Jack made another $10 bet. Again, he was dealt a Blackjack. Time to walk away.

"Whew, I better not push my luck!" Jack said with a fake smile as he tipped the dealer a $5 chip. The dealer thanked him as Jack collected the rest of his chips and stuffed them in his pocket.

Jack wandered over to a Roulette table with several people lazily dropping chips here and there. He watched a few spins, then, still standing and casually half-turned away from the table, he dropped two $5 chips on Black. Twenty-nine won; a Black number, which meant Jack had just doubled his money. He stacked the four $5 chips into one small pile, and pushed it over to Red. The croupier spun the ball again, more bets were placed by the other players, and the ball dropped down into 18, Red. The croupier paid out $20 to Jack, who collected his chips and walked off.

Jack had just won $24 at Blackjack, and another $30 at Roulette, all without losing a penny. His actions and winnings were not even remotely out-of-the-ordinary as far as the casino was concerned, but Jack wanted to run one more test on the slot machines. In order to completely allay any suspicions that may even remotely be coming his way, he stopped at the bar for a good hour and had a couple of drinks while watching a baseball game on TV.

After paying the bartender, Jack walked over to the slot machines and found a bank of penny slots in a back corner with no one around. He took the other $20 bill out of his pocket and fed it into one of the machines, an Egyptian-themed job with a crappy payout chart. Jack bet the absolute minimum: one penny. He pressed the button to spin the digital reels, and won $3, the maximum amount possible for this machine on a one penny bet.

He repeated this one-penny bet nine more times, and every time he won the maximum $3 payout. Jack cashed out his winnings and looked at the ticket. He had turned $20 into $50, while putting only ten cents on the line. Jack was satisfied that his powers were still intact, at least for now. He had also all but confirmed that not only was it impossible for him to lose, it seemed that when he won, it was the maximum possible win for that specific betting situation.

This was something Jack had suspected since winning at the gas station, but needed more information to confirm. He didn't just win his Blackjack hands; he won *with* Blackjack, both times. He didn't just win money with that lottery ticket; he won the maximum available for that game. He would have to be very careful about what games he played and how much he bet.

Satisfied with his tests, Jack cashed out his chips and slot ticket, and had dinner at a casino restaurant before turning in for the night. Tomorrow was going to be a big day, and he had to get some rest. He would be arriving in Las Vegas tomorrow afternoon, and he still had a lot of planning to do before hitting the tables.

Chapter Four

The next afternoon, Jack pulled up to the valet stand at the most expensive hotel on the Vegas Strip. The valet took his car, and Jack walked inside the lobby of the hotel carrying his only luggage – a small duffel bag stuffed with a week's worth of clothes, some bathroom supplies, and about $12,000 in cash. He walked up to the check-in desk, handed the clerk his license, a credit card, and a twenty-dollar bill, and asked if any rooms were available without a reservation.

The clerk, a black woman in her 30's, took Jack's money and cards without hesitation, and started clacking away on the computer. There was a room available, and a fairly nice one at that, at a very reasonable price. Jack wasn't sure if it was the $20 that got him the room, or the fact that he was in Vegas in the middle of the week during the off-season.

He had a corner room on the 27th floor overlooking the Strip. This was probably the nicest room Jack had ever stayed in during all of his trips to Vegas, but then again, he usually played it frugal and spent most of his money on the casino floor instead of fancy hotel rooms. This time he made an exception.

Jack sat down at the desk, grabbed the complimentary pen and paper, and removed the cash and his cell phone from his duffel bag. He opened up the calculator app on his phone and got to work. He planned on staying in Vegas for three more full days, and would see how far he could push his luck while staying under the radar. Just before crossing the border into Nevada, he believed he hit on the perfect solution – Baccarat.

Baccarat was a card game steeped in tradition, etiquette, and superstition. It would not be out of the ordinary at all to make weird, random, high dollar bets at a Baccarat table. Jack's plan was to first find a table filled with Asian players, the more superstitious and rowdier the better. Traditionally speaking, the player with the biggest bet at the table decides how he will bet, and then the rest of the players follow suit, betting along with him. So, Jack would simply wait for the big bettor to place his bet, and then bet the same thing.

The genius in this move is that no one would suspect *him* of anything, since he was merely following along with the other players. Also, if there are other players at a Baccarat table, one doesn't need to bet on every single hand. Jack would simply sit around for five or ten hands, pretend to track the game looking for patterns, act like he's making crucial decisions, and then place a bet along with the big better at random intervals. If he kept his bet levels well below most of the other players, no one would even give him a second thought.

In order for this plan to work, Jack would need the perfect table. After freshening up, he made a round of the casino floor to get the lay of the land. Every once in a while, he stopped at a low-value slot machine and made a few bets at the absolute minimum, just to make sure his powers still worked in Vegas. They did. He used the $70 he made doing this experiment to treat himself to dinner, then decided to check out the high limit room.

The high limit room of the casino was where the high rollers liked to play, and it was where all the serious Baccarat action would be found. Jack found a Baccarat table with three middle-aged Asian men, all dressed in polo shirts and khaki slacks, and stood about ten feet off to the side to watch them play.

The goal in Baccarat is get a two or three card total higher than the dealer's, and as close to nine as possible. Unlike Blackjack, you can't "go over" in Baccarat; if you score higher than a nine, say, a 13, the tens digit is simply dropped and you would end up with a three. You also don't get to decide whether to take an extra card or not. There are strict rules that determine if a card is drawn or if the hand stands. Furthermore, the entire table plays one hand against the dealer's one hand. There is no individual play in Baccarat, unless you are playing alone.

The only real decisions to be made in Baccarat are how much to bet, and where. You can bet on "Player" or "Banker." These don't correspond to the actual players at the table or the casino banking the game; it is simply the names given to the two possible bets. Two cards are initially dealt to Player and Banker, and the player at the table with the highest bet in each has the honor of revealing the cards and determining which side has won.

Despite all of this, many players like to believe they have some sort of control over the game in one way or another. Jack would use this to his advantage, and pretend to be a highly superstitious player. Above every Baccarat table, there is a TV screen detailing the results of every hand of a Baccarat shoe. Jack would pretend to scrutinize these results, also called the Road Maps, in an attempt to find patterns and trends in order to decide his bets. Many players also liked to keep track of results on score cards provided by the casino.

The Asian trio were betting about $200-$400 each per hand. Not a bad amount for Jack's purposes, but he was hoping for a little richer game; at least $800 per hand from the other players. Jack watched the dealer pull four cards out of the shoe and give two to what was presumably the big bettor. Jack readjusted his view of the table and actually saw the man had a stack of five black chips in front of him – a bet of $500. The man slowly peeled up the corner of one of his cards and said something to his compatriots. He flipped the card over and revealed a seven. He took the other card, grabbed it with both hands, and slowly but forcefully started peeling up the long side of the card, revealing fractions of a millimeter of it at a time. He whooped and immediately flipped the card over, revealing a face card. The Asians had a grand total of seven; not a bad hand.

The dealer flipped over his two cards and revealed a four and a two, for a total of six. The rules dictated he had to stand, so he was not able to draw a third card in an attempt to beat the three Asians. The dealer paid out the winning bets, and the players began pointing at the Road Map readout and speaking in what Jack was sure was a Chinese dialect.

Another hand was played, but this time the three players lost. Jack decided to make another round of the casino floor, maybe have another drink or two, and let the Baccarat action heat up a little before jumping in to execute his plan. As he turned towards the exit of the high limit room, he almost bumped directly into two more Asian men wearing polos and khaki slacks.

"Whoop…'scuse me!" Jack said as he smiled and pivoted to let the two gentlemen pass. They smiled back and curtly bowed their heads before heading to join the three other players at the table. Jack almost continued out of the high limit room but was stopped by the raucous cheers greeting the two newcomers. He turned back to watch.

A joyous cacophony of the Chinese language erupted from the five men at the table, with handshakes and back pats being traded all around. Judging from their dress, Jack assumed they either all worked for the same company, or were in town for some sort of convention. Their attitudes indicated that maybe they were celebrating some sort of big deal that had come to fruition. Several men in suits, employees of the casino, also appeared out of nowhere and rallied around the table.

Again, Jack almost turned to leave before noticing that the dealer was pushing several stacks of very high-dollar chips towards one of the newcomers as he was signing a piece of paper handed to him by one of the men in suits. The chips were brown, also called "chocolates," and Jack knew that meant they were worth $5,000 apiece. The man had two and a half stacks of chips in front of him, meaning he had a quarter of a million dollars in chips ready to play with. The second newcomer was also signing a piece of paper, and the dealer pushed two stacks of chocolate chips in front of him - $200,000. The three other men were buying in for more chips as well, but not nearly as much. Their stacks were full of blacks and purples - $100 and $500 chips, respectively. A cocktail waitress appeared, and a round of drinks was ordered.

Jack instantly became very nervous. This would be the perfect table to enact his plan; five, raucous, drunk men, betting huge amounts of money. From the way the first three men had played, Jack deduced they were probably also the type to follow trends and superstitions. A woman in a suit locked eyes with Jack for a few seconds, and he was suddenly aware that he had just been standing around for several long minutes ogling some very rich men. He didn't want to arouse any suspicions whatsoever, so he reached into his jacket pocket and removed $10,000 in cash.

He walked up to the Baccarat table while the players were still talking to each other and plunked his money down in front of the dealer. Jack sat down at the far end of the table, with one empty seat to his right between him and the first Chinese player, the one who had bought in for $250,000, and whom Jack now dubbed in his mind as "High Roller." Jack asked for purple chips, and the dealer counted out his ten grand before pushing a stack of twenty $500 chips out in front of him. Jack grabbed a complimentary scorecard and pen and began to fictitiously study the digital Road Map display at the far end of the table.

Other than some cursory glances and brief smiles, the Chinese players ignored him. A few more minutes went by and Jack wondered when the hell these guys were going to start playing. His whole plan depended on other people making the first move. High Roller eventually pointed at the Road Maps and said something, and grabbed three chips from his stack - $15,000. He confidently smacked them down on the betting circle marked Banker. The four other Chinese immediately bet varying amounts on Banker. Jack grabbed a lone $500 chip from his stack and followed suit.

Here we go.

The dealer dealt four cards from the shoe, pushed two to High Roller and kept two for himself. A hush descended over the table. High Roller slowly and agonizingly began peeling up the short edge of the card, exposing it bit by bit. He let out a heavy sigh that Jack thought might also have been a swear word in Chinese. The card was flipped over, revealing a two. High Roller then grabbed the second card, and repeated the peeling process. Jack knew what the card would be – a seven. That would give the table a total of nine, the best possible hand, and a winner. If it was anything other than a seven, that would mean Jack's powers were no longer working.

High Roller announced some information gleaned from looking at the short end of the card, and the other four players began chanting something in their native language. The card was turned flat on the table by ninety degrees, and High Roller began slowly peeling up the long end of the card. The chanting became louder and louder, and Jack just wanted High Roller to turn over the god damned card and reveal a seven. After a few painful seconds, High Roller did just that – Jack and the five Chinese players had a total of nine.

Everyone cheered, and the dealer moved to turn over his two cards. Only a total of nine would save him now and end the coup in a tie, but he flipped over two threes, adding up to six. The table cheered again, and the dealer paid everyone their winning bets.

Jack breathed a sigh of relief. Either he got incredibly lucky, or his powers were still well-intact and functioning. The next step in his plan was to simply sit out several hands, in order to make it look like he was studying the results and waiting for the absolute perfect time to bet. This would not be an unusual strategy at all in a game of high stakes Baccarat, and should not attract much attention. A cocktail waitress appeared, and Jack ordered a cognac while the Chinese players placed their wagers. Jack indicated to the dealer he would be sitting out this hand, and the cards were dealt.

Over the next four hands, the Chinese players all bet together, following the lead of High Roller. They won two hands, and lost two, and High Roller spent an especially long time studying the Road Maps for the next hand. He finally dropped $20,000 in chips on the circle marked Player. The other four mimicked his decision, and this time Jack did as well; another $500 chip.

The Player cards were pushed towards High Roller, and he began the process of slowly and methodically turning them over. Jack knew the total would be a nine, it just came down to what the individual cards would be. This time the table had a four and a five, and Jack collected another $500.

He decided to sit out five hands this time, nursing his cognac, and fastidiously "studying" the Road Maps to plot his next move. The way these Chinese fellows played, it took them a good five or six minutes to finish a coup, so Jack was left twiddling his thumbs for almost half an hour before betting again. He wanted the casino to forget about him, to focus on the big Asian gamblers, to just think he was some random guy playing a "system."

More importantly, he needed the casino to forget about his bets, and whether or not he had won or lost. Jack knew casinos kept track of the chips in front of the player, and liked to type a rough count of their totals in their computers every once in a while. In a crude attempt to thwart this as much as possible, Jack was constantly fiddling with his chips, stacking them and restacking them into different sized piles, and even palming two or three of them in his hand for several minutes at time.

Jack jumped back into the action while the Chinese players were on a hot streak. They had just won three Banker hands in a row, and High Roller dropped $50,000 onto the Banker circle in front him. The other players pushed chips onto Banker as well, and this time Jack squared up two $500 chips to bet with the table. The dealer slid two cards to High Roller, and he began the dance.

The first card flipped over was a nine, and Jack instantly knew the other card would be a ten. In Baccarat, a ten would effectively count as a zero, giving the table a total of nine and a winning hand. One of the Chinese men started pounding the table and shouting "Monkey!" and the other players joined in to the chorus. In Baccarat, a Monkey was a face card, equaling ten.

Jack began chanting "Monkey" as well, and then he had a sudden flash of inspiration. He randomly thought of a face card - the Jack of Hearts - in his mind's eye, and with each round of "Monkey," he imagined the card pulsing brighter and brighter in his head.

Monkey! Jack of Hearts.

Monkey! JACK OF HEARTS.

Monkey! **JACK OF HEARTS.**

High Roller slowly began peeling up the edge of the second card, paused for a moment, then laid it back flat on the table. He then closes his eyes and began laughing. The other players stopped chanting and just looked at him. High Roller flipped the card over, revealing a Jack of Hearts.

Oh, shit.

Chapter Five

Jack's head began to swirl. Did he really cause the Jack of Hearts to appear? Or was it pure chance? Numbers began running through Jack's head. Assuming his winning powers were foolproof, that meant he *knew* the card would definitely total 10. In Baccarat, there were 16 unique cards in a deck equaling 10 – the 10, the Jack, the Queen, and the King – four ranks of four suits each. This meant Jack had a one in 16 chance of guessing the Jack of Hearts.

Considering his newfound powers, though, he wasn't so sure of that. In the last two days, he had never actually tried to "control" the specific outcome of a game. He simply placed a bet and the universe let him win. Did he also have the power to control *how* he won? He needed to run another test.

The other players, wanting to continue their hot streak, immediately bet on Banker after the casino paid out everyone's winnings. Jack put another $1000 on the Banker circle in front of him. The cards were dealt, and High Roller started peeling. Jack thought of another card and focused all of his concentration on the image in his mind.

Ace of Clubs.

ACE OF CLUBS.

ACE OF CLUBS.

High Roller turned over the Ace of Clubs. The Chinese men collectively breathed out and sat back in their chairs before all speaking up simultaneously and rallying around their leader. High Roller rubbed his hands together and began work on the second card. This time, Jack pictured the Eight of Diamonds.

Eight of Diamonds.

EIGHT OF DIAMONDS.

EIGHT OF DIAMONDS.

High Roller exploded with a stream of fervent Chinese and flipped over his second card – the Eight of Diamonds. Jack was nauseous, and his mouth suddenly dried. Ultimately, this newfound discovery in his powers didn't change the overall plan, but Jack didn't like it… it gave him *too* much power. Simply winning every single time just felt like being really lucky, and was a power he could handle. But actually being able to *control* the specific outcome of an event, however… that was too godlike. He didn't want that much responsibility. This might end up being a curse after all.

Jack suddenly felt angry at whatever cosmic being had gifted him with this ability. Okay, he thought, I'm done. I've made a decent little chunk of money, and I appreciate that, but you can have these powers back. Party's over. I want to be normal again.

Another cognac appeared in front of Jack, and he couldn't remember if he had actually ordered it or not. He tipped the waitress a green $25 chip, and she thanked him before doling out drinks to the other players.

Jack had another idea. High Roller and his crew again bet on Banker, but Jack refrained from betting this time. Two cards were dealt to High Roller, and he began the slow reveal. Jack concentrated and pictured a card in his mind.

Six of Spades.

SIX OF SPADES.

SIX OF SPADES.

High Roller turned over the card and revealed the Four of Hearts. With this bit of information, Jack concluded that this power may only work if he actually had money on the line. High Roller's other card was the Two of Diamonds. The table had a total of six, not a bad total, but also not great. The dealer flipped over his two cards revealing a pair of twos, giving him a total of four. According to the rules, he had to draw a third card in this scenario, and he pulled a three. This gave him a total of seven, beating the Chinese players.

They groaned and the dealer swept away enough chips to buy a house.

By now Jack was sweating so he removed his jacket. High Roller and Gang feverishly debated their plan of attack while Jack stared off into space and took some deep breathes. He had one last thing he wanted to try. When High Roller slid $20,000 onto the Player circle, the rest of the table slid their bets in as well, including Jack. The cards were dealt, and High Roller cracked his knuckles and started to work his mojo. Jack concentrated and pictured the Queen of Hearts.

Queen of Hearts.

QUEEN OF HEARTS.

QUEEN OF HEARTS.

High Roller revealed the Queen of Hearts to the rest of the table. Jack concentrated again.

Ten of Spades.

TEN OF SPADES.

TEN OF SPADES.

High Roller cursed and flipped over the Ten of Spades. The players at the table had a total score of zero. The dealer turned over his cards and revealed a total of seven. The coup was not over yet, as the players were obligated to take another card before the final decision was made. The dealer pushed a sole card over to High Roller, and the Chinese started screaming for a winning card. Jack realized he had been holding his breath, and he continued to hold it while concentrating…

King of Clubs.

KING OF CLUBS.

KING OF CLUBS.

High Roller pounded his fist on the edge of the table in anger, and ripped the card in half. Jack looked down at the piece that landed in front of his chip stack and saw the King of Clubs starting back up at him. He exhaled heavily and took several deep breaths. The table had a zero. They had lost. Jack had lost. For the first time since acquiring his powers, he had lost. He pushed the remainder of his chips towards the dealer and asked to color up while the Chinese crew deliberated and argued with each other while pointing at the Road Maps.

The dealer gave Jack two chocolate chips, two yellow chips ("bananas") and several smaller denomination chips. After tipping the cocktail waitress and the dealer, and paying the 5% commission owed on winning Banker hands, Jack had cleared over $2,000 in less than an hour. He stuffed the chips in his pocket, grabbed his jacket, and left the high limit room.

Jack aimlessly wandered the casino floor while his mind raced. Within moments, everything had changed. If he did nothing, he won automatically. If he concentrated, he could dictate exactly *how* he would win. Furthermore, he could also control exactly how he would *lose*. His original plan was thrown out the window, as he now no longer had to worry about winning too much or disguising his play. He could win or lose as he pleased, and as long as he never got too greedy, no one would be the wiser.

Wait a minute… he had just lost, but he hadn't continued to play to see if he could actually still win. Frantically, he stopped at the nearest gaming table, a Craps table, and fished a $25 chip out of his pocket. Several players were in the midst of a heated roll, and when they Sevened-out, the croupiers swept a table full of chips away and new bets were placed. Jack dropped his $25 chip on the Pass Line, and a portly balding man with a mustache picked up the dice and threw them across the table.

His first roll was a Seven, which meant Jack had won his Pass Line bet. He pressed his bet, leaving $50 on the Pass Line. Mustache rolled the dice, and again hit a Seven. Jack's money doubled to $100, and still he let it ride. Mustache's third roll tumbled down the felt to finish on Seven, and Jack was now staring down at $200. So, he could still win. Now the next test.

He picked up $150 from the felt, leaving $50 still on the Pass Line. Mustache began his fourth roll, but this time Jack was concentrating on the number two, which would be a losing roll. He kept repeating the number two in his head, "two, two, two," and Mustache and the other players let out a collective groan when the dice stopped on Two. One of the croupiers swept away Jack's $50 in chips and the other players started placing more bets. Jack needed a drink.

He walked to one of the casino bars and ordered a Pina Colada. It was cool and refreshing, and Jack closed his eyes and took several sips while trying to calm himself. He was basically a superhero now. He could control the outcome of games of chance in which he had a personal stake. He wondered how far it would go.

If he bet somebody that a plane would crash, would hundreds of people die simply because he had ten bucks riding on it? Could he wager on the next Presidential election, both for the United States and multiple other countries, and control the fate of the world? Could he have people assassinated? What if he asked the bartender right now, "Hey, I betcha a dollar that Kim Jong-Un is dead in the next five minutes?" What would happen? Could he "gamble" people back from the dead? Could he "gamble" that he would live for a thousand years?

Jacked opened his eyes and just zoned out staring at the back of the bar while sipping his drink. An hour and another Pina Colada later, he decided not to focus on how much control he had over the fate of the universe, and instead worried about the fate of his own life. He tipped the bartender, very generously, and headed back into the high limit room.

Chapter Six

Jack was convinced that Baccarat was still currently the best bet for exploiting his powers. There's a reason it's the favorite game of high rollers. Massive bets and wild swings in wins and losses are de rigueur for Baccarat, the most popular casino game in the world. He could slowly ramp up his wins over the next few days, losing when necessary, and by the end of his trip he could be betting $100,000 a hand. By early next week Jack would be a millionaire. The casino wouldn't like it, but they would just attribute their loss to an incredible run of luck. Vegas had seen wild swings like that before, and they would again. The casino would be eager to invite Jack back to Vegas and roll out the red carpet in an effort to win their money back.

Back in the high limit room, the Chinese team was gone, but several other tables had a smattering of players. Jack pulled the high-dollar chips out of his pocket, and walked up to an empty table. He put the two bananas firmly in the Banker circle and waited while the dealer completed the ritual of discarding several cards at the beginning of the dealing shoe and then dealing out the hands.

Jack let himself win the first three hands, so he could have some decent capital to work with, and then ping-ponged between winning and losing for the next several hours. He found a good groove, one that he felt avoided any suspicion, and by six o'clock in the morning he was up almost $200,000. It could have easily been more, but he wanted to throw in a few big $50,000 losses at the last minute to make it look like he was going on tilt.

It was unavoidable that big play like this would catch the attention of the casino suits, and Jack was prepared for that. After all, he had nothing to hide. Nothing, that is, that could be proven in a court of law. A VIP host introduced himself as a Mr. Frank Fitzgerald, and Jack willfully provided him with any info he asked for. Mr. Fitzgerald comped Jack food and beverage for the rest of his stay and upgraded his hotel room. Jack deposited his winnings in the casino cage and was taking a shower in his new hotel room by seven in the morning.

He needed some sleep. As he lay in bed on the verge of dreamland, he remembered why he was even here in the first place. He had been fired, and his former company, Motley Rivers, was probably going to come under investigation for some serious financial crimes. A sudden paranoia crept into his head, and he wondered if he had set himself up for failure.

The police or FBI or whoever would see Jack Cross, former employee of a crooked company, heading to Vegas the day after being fired and winning hundreds of thousands of dollars. There's no reality where that wasn't incredibly suspicious. Jack had sworn that he wouldn't do anything to draw attention to himself, and in less than two days he had gotten greedy and thrown that out the window.

He shouldn't have won so much money right off the bat. It was dangerous. He had to make some adjustments on the fly and start planning ahead. He couldn't just plan for the next hand of Baccarat, though, or even just the rest of his trip. He had to start planning months if not years ahead of time to make sure he would stay safe and sound. He batted around a few ideas, and then drifted off to sleep.

When Jack awoke, it was early afternoon. He decided on a game plan for the rest of his Vegas trip. Today, he would lose back a good chunk of his winnings from yesterday, maybe around $150,000. Then, tomorrow, he would win back about $50,000, and on the last day, a big win of $200,000.

That would "only" put him ahead about $100,000 of where he was right now, and a total win of around $300,000 in three and a half days of gambling. That was a completely reasonable swing for a high rolling Baccarat player. Coincidentally, that last day would also be his 53rd birthday, so he might as well go out with a bang.

Jack got ready and went down to the casino floor to get some lunch before hitting the tables. The high limit room was fairly empty, and he sat down alone at a table. If he did say so himself, he played well the part of a superstitious high rolling Baccarat player. He gambled until dinner, then for a few hours afterwards. He was still worn out from yesterday, and he went to bed shortly before 11pm. Jack's plan was still perfectly on track; his tally for the day was a loss of $160,000.

The next day Jack decided to play it even safer, only winning back about $20,000 overall after a good twelve hours of play. He was really starting to enjoy the high roller lifestyle. If these powers lasted forever, he could see himself becoming a professional gambler. Win $2,000,000 this year, lose $1,000,000 the next, drinking $200 bottles of champagne in a 5,000 square foot hotel room, free of charge… All while donating a large chunk to charity, of course. Jack had already started thinking about starting some sort of charitable foundation.

On the last day that Jack was scheduled to be in Vegas, he received a phone call. He was halfway through his gambling day, and up about $70,000, when a Special Agent Rick Michaels from the FBI called and wanted to know if he could come in and answer some questions about Motley Rivers, LLC.

Wow, thought Jack, they're working fast. Jack told the Agent he would have no problems with that, but he would need a few days to get back to town and, of course, hire a lawyer. Jack had absolutely nothing to hide, but he also wanted to make sure his rights weren't being violated.

To celebrate his birthday, Jack half-jokingly asked his host if he could bring him a birthday cake. To his surprise, Frank complied, and an hour later, a hotel chef appeared pushing a dessert cart laden with a red velvet cake covered in chocolate icing. There was enough cake for Jack, Frank, the chef, every dealer in the high limit room, and several other gamblers to have a piece, and everyone sang Happy Birthday to Jack.

Later that night as he was packing his bags to drive out early the next morning, Frank called and invited him to come back to play next month. Everything would be taken care of, even a round trip plane ticket. All Jack had to do was bring money to gamble with; preferably the $300,000 he had just spent the last three days winning from the casino. Jack agreed to return, and Frank made the necessary arrangements.

On the drive back home, Jack thought about the investigation, and wondered about finding a lawyer. He saw plenty of ads for lawyers who knew how to handle DUIs, workplace injuries, and divorces, but not about Federal white-collar financial crimes. Even though he was completely innocent, he still wanted a really good lawyer, just in case, and now he could afford one.

When he arrived home, Colonel Hacker was surprised to see him back early, and then warned him that several Federal agents had been prowling around the neighborhood the last day or so, questioning the neighbors about one Jack Cross. This surprised Jack, as he figured they just wanted ask him if he knew anything about any shady goings-on at Motley Rivers. What the Colonel had told him made it sound like he was more than just a potential witness, though.

Hacker also had some good news, however. He was good friends with one of the best criminal defense attorneys in the state, a man by the name of Gary Stephens. Mr. Stephens had spent an entire military career as an officer in JAG, or Judge Advocate General. After retiring from the military's legal system, he started his own law practice specializing in white collar crimes.

Jack contacted Stephens and made an appointment to meet with him the very next day. Jack took every scrap of paperwork he could find relating to Motley Rivers, including paystubs going back over eight years. He even went through his personal email accounts to see if there was anything he should archive or print out.

Gary Stephens' office was a literal mansion. He and his team worked out of a turn-of-the-20th century estate house decorated with ornate wood carvings and draped in tapestries and red velvet. In the conference room, Jack laid out everything he knew, including the $10,000 bonus and brief conversation with the security guard. Stephens seemed completely satisfied that Jack would have nothing to worry about, and they both climbed into Stephens luxury sedan to drive to the FBI's field office.

Jack Cross and Gary Stephens sat in the FBI's small conference room, which was not nearly as impressive as Stephens'. They had been waiting for over an hour, which

Stephens said was highly unusual. Jack had just asked if they should just get up and leave, when a Special Agent entered the room. He appeared very flustered, and his mustached face was red and sweaty.

"Mr. Cross?"

"Yes?" replied Jack.

"I'm Special Agent Michaels, FBI."

Stephens immediately stood up to shake the agent's hand.

"I'm Gary Stephens, Mr. Cross' counsel."

"Mr. Stephens," Agent Michaels said as they shook hands. Stephens and Agent Michaels both sat down.

"Mr. Cross… Mr. Stephens. We've had some interesting turns of event the last few hours. As you're already aware, we wanted to talk to you about your former place of employment, Motley Rivers, LLC."

"Yes. I don't really know anything. I had just heard—" Stephens held up his hand to stop Jack from talking.

Stephens turned to the Agent and said, "You were saying, Agent Michaels?"

"Um, yes," Agent Michaels mumbled. "Well, the day after you were fired, your former executives turned over thousands of pages of documents implicating you in some serious financial crimes, including wire fraud and embezzlement."

"Embezzlement?" questioned Stephens.

"Yes…almost ten million dollars over the last three years."

"That's bullshit!" Jack shouted. Stephens put a reassuring hand on Jack's forearm to calm him.

Agent Michaels resumed speaking. "Well, yes, I mean that was last week. But, uh…as I mentioned, there have been some…"

Stephens picked up where the Agent had trailed off, "…interesting turns of event?"

"Yes," said Agent Michaels. "I'll just get right to the point. Late last night, every single shred of evidence in this case was either destroyed or has disappeared. All hard copies of documents were burned to ashes in a mysterious fire in the evidence room. Every file on every computer, hard drive, thumb drive, CD, and even two floppy discs, if you can believe that, has been deleted. All recovery efforts have failed. I mean, we're the FBI. We have the best guys in the business. It's like these files never existed, except in our memories. We even located two offshore bank accounts in your name, each with almost $5,000,000 in them. Now, the money and

59

those accounts have both vanished. No one can find any trace that they ever existed."

Stephens cautiously spoke up, "Surely you're not now implicating Mr. Cross in the destruction of all this evidence?"

Agent Michaels held up his hands. "Oh, no, no, in fact, quite the opposite. You see, also, sometime between midnight and three o'clock this morning, the president of the company, as well as three vice presidents, all committed suicide in their homes. They all left suicide notes confessing to wire fraud and embezzlement of almost ten million dollars, and completely exonerating you by name."

Jack and Stephens looked at each other in astonishment and confusion. Agent Michaels continued.

"So…in light of there being no evidence of any crimes ever having been committed, and even if there *was* evidence, four other people have already confessed, and then killed themselves… you're free to go. Thank you for your time." Agent Michaels stood up and left the room.

Jack couldn't believe what he was hearing. Those bastards were going to set him up. In fact, they *had* set him up. Who knows how long they had been doctoring evidence and forging documents? They were going to frame him to take the fall for whatever crooked shit they had been doing. But why? He was a nobody at Motley Rivers. He worked to live, he didn't live to work. He wasn't a threat to anyone. He didn't care about promotions or office politics. Just give him a steady job and a decent pay raise every year or two and he was happy.

Then again, maybe that's why they chose him. Because he *was* a nobody. Just a pawn that could be sacrificed for… whatever reason. The whole thing still didn't make sense, but now it sounded like it may never make sense because every last bit of evidence was gone.

As Jack and Stephens headed out of the field office, Stephens' phone rang and he ducked into an alcove to answer it. Jack's mouth was dry as a bone, so he spent a good half minute at a water fountain in the lobby. As he stood up to wipe his mouth, Agent Michaels appeared out of nowhere and approached him.

"Mr. Cross?"

"Yes?"

"I don't know what the hell happened here. We're going to be talking about this at the Bureau for months, if not years. I don't think our bosses in D.C. are too happy about this."

61

"Well…" Jack had to choose his words carefully. "I'm sorry to hear that."

"I just want you know, if you somehow were mixed up in this, you got really lucky. And if you weren't mixed up in it…. Well, still consider yourself really lucky. Either way, keep your nose clean. I don't think I can handle another case like this."

Agent Michaels started to walk away, but Jack stopped him.

"Agent Michaels… will the suicide notes be released publicly?"

"Oh, not for a while," chortled Agent Michaels. "That's the only evidence we have anything even happened. We'll be poring over those things with a microscope for weeks."

Agent Michaels walked off, and Jack Cross and Gary Stephens left the field office. As they drove back to Stephens' office, Stephens was going on and on about how that meeting was one of the craziest things he had ever been a part of. Jack was only half-listening, staring out the window and thinking about everything that had happened in the last week and a half.

Agent Michaels said the suicide notes were the only remaining evidence that a crime had been committed. He was mostly right, but there was one other thing he didn't know about. Nobody knew about it, not even Jack's lawyer.

On his last day in Vegas, after the FBI had called him and asked if he could come in to talk, he went up to his room, sat down at the desk, and wrote a letter on the hotel stationary. A letter to himself. He then handed the letter, with a $100 tip, to a front desk clerk and asked him to mail it to his house.

When Jack got home after the meeting with the FBI, he went over to the Colonel's house to get the mail his neighbor had been collecting for him while he had been out of town. In all the commotion and talk about Federal Agents and lawyers, he had forgotten to get it the day before. In the stack of junk mail and bills, there was the letter he mailed himself, addressed to Jack Cross, with a return address reading, "Jack Cross, Vegas Baby!"

Jack tore open the envelope and read the letter.

"I, Jack Cross, bet myself, Jack Cross, one U.S. dollar, that I will never be in any danger or legal trouble as a result of my affiliation with Motley Rivers, LLC."

He took a single dollar bill out of the envelope with his right hand, took it with his left hand, and put it in his pocket. He smiled.

"You win, Jack."

Voices

Chapter One

The President of the United States of America sat at his desk in the Oval Office re-reading the previous day's intelligence brief. The bowtie of his tuxedo was undone, and a pocket square was casually tossed on his desk. He had just gotten back from a dinner with some foreign diplomats, and he wanted to double-check something a Saudi official had told him over a delicious crème brulee.

The door to the office suddenly burst open, and a flurry of suits and military uniforms entered the room. The President, startled, looked up to see the Chairman of the Joint Chiefs of Staff, the Chief of Staff of the Air Force, the Chief of Staff of the Space Force, and the Administrator and Deputy Administrator of NASA hurriedly walking to the front of his desk, where they all stopped.

"Jesus, what the hell is going on?" asked the President.

"Mr. President," the Chairman spoke up, "We've lost contact with the Norgay. We think it's something serious."

The U.S.S. Tenzing Norgay was a deep space survey ship that had been orbiting Mars for the last several weeks. Its mission was to scan and map every square millimeter of the planet's surface in order to determine the best location to build the first permanent manned bases on Mars. NASA had already built several temporary outposts where astronauts had spent several months at a time performing experiments and learning how to live on the Red Planet, but those posts had been abandoned for almost a year. NASA felt they had garnered enough information to go whole hog and start building permanent structures. The locations of the temporary outposts were obviously not chosen randomly, but after spending months with boots on the ground, NASA discovered they were not exactly ideal locations, either.

The Norgay's job was to scan the surface with state-of-the-art geographic deep space survey equipment, which included cameras advanced enough to read 12-point type from orbit in almost complete darkness. Also onboard were multiple-wavelength seismic distance scanners, which could, also from orbit, penetrate the surface and determine the chemical and physical composition of the ground down to almost 20 meters.

The crew of the U.S.S. Tenzing Norgay consisted of five people. The military members of the crew were the Commander of the ship, the Pilot, and a Co-Pilot/Engineer.

Also onboard were two civilian Mission Specialists; an astro-geographer and an imagery specialist.

The Norgay's job was supposed to be a simple one. Going to Mars was almost old hat at this point. Men had been walking on its surface off and on for several years, and manned missions to the surface or to orbit barely made the news anymore. Every inch of its surface had been scanned and photographed ten times over by now, but not with the advanced equipment the Norgay was carrying. Simple as its job was to be, it was still an important one. NASA needed this data if it was going to move forward with permanent bases where men, and even families, would be spending years, if not entire lives.

The Chairman spoke up. "Mr. President, three hours ago, the Norgay sent a brief message. All it said was, 'We're under attack. Going dark.'"

"Under attack? From whom?"

"We don't know, Mr. President. We haven't heard anything from them since, and we've lost all sensor readings and communications with them."

"What does that mean?" asked the President. "Has the ship been destroyed?"

Now the NASA Administrator spoke up. "Not necessarily, Mr. President. They said they were 'going dark.' It's possible the Norgay has simply shut down the majority of their systems and is running solely on life support and an absolute minimum of computer power to keep the basic functions running. From any appreciable distance, it would look as if they had just vanished into thin air. We wouldn't even be able to locate them with our remote equipment on Mars, let alone from here on Earth."

"So," continued the Chairman, "we're hoping they've shut down in an attempt to 'hide' from whomever was attacking them."

"Where are the Chinese?" asked the President. "Aren't they mining the Belt right now?"

The China National Space Administration currently had a small fleet of drone ships mining an area of the Main Asteroid Belt, in an effort to locate precious metals and other valuable resources. The Main Asteroid Belt was located approximately 286 million miles from Earth, and 200 million miles past Mars.

"Yes, sir," answered the Chief of Staff of the Space Force. "But they're on the other side of the Sun this time of year. Not even remotely close to Mars."

The President continued his queries. "Who else is out there right now? Do we have any leads?"

The Space Force Chief continued, "Europe and China both have probes on Mercury. Europe also has two men still orbiting Venus. India currently has two probes en route to Jupiter and Saturn, roughly in the Norgay's neck of the woods. Russia is still doing retrofits so they have nobody past the I.S.S. And of course, we all have crews on the Moon right now. Nobody has reported any unusual activity in the last 24 hours, at least nothing that we've been able to pick up."

The President nodded and thought for a second. "Does anyone else know about the Norgay's message?"

The Chairman looked at his watch and said, "By now? Probably everyone. They sent it out so fast they didn't have time to encode it. Even if they had, we couldn't have kept this quiet for more than a day, anyway."

"Dammit," said the President as he stood up. "Okay, double check with India, see if those two probes have picked anything up since this morning."

It was going to be a long night, with lots of phone calls being made all across the world, and transmissions being sent from one corner of the Inner Solar System to the other.

The Norgay's last message was transmitted through the Martian Surface Relay System, or MSRS, which meant they were currently on the dark side of the planet, out of sight of every available telescope, and using surface equipment to bounce a message from the far side back to Earth.

For the next week, the "disappearance" of the U.S.S. Tenzing Norgay, and her cryptic last message, was the biggest news story in the world. America's political foes vehemently denied any involvement in the supposed attack, and, in fact, China offered to redirect some of their Main Belt drones to Mars to investigate. Of course, it would take months for the drones to arrive, considering how far away they were.

The first of India's probes was already too far past the Main Belt to be of any help, but the second probe had actually been close enough to catch something interesting. Around the time that the Norgay had sent their distress call, the probe detected a brief anomalous energy signature, or surge, coming from somewhere between Mars and the Main Belt. No human craft were in the area, and, according to scientists, there were no naturally occurring phenomena that could produce such a signature. Several seconds later, there was another energy surge, this time extremely close to Mars. The energy surges were all anyone currently had to go on, so they were studied intensely.

Another key piece of information that the world latched onto was the fact that the Norgay had not orbited back around from the dark side of Mars. This meant one of two things: the Norgay had either been destroyed, or they were actually holding their orbit on the far side of the planet for some reason, precariously and constantly perched between the surface and deep space, in near total darkness.

In the meantime, a rescue mission was being planned. Naturally, such missions were already mostly planned, at least on paper, so as to be ready to go at a moment's notice. As luck would have it, the European Space Agency had just finished construction on a new high-speed supply freighter, the E.S.S. Heeren. This new class of freighter was designed to run 20% faster than any other freighter currently in use, and could hold almost 30% more cargo. Being just days away from test launch when the Norgay disappeared, it could have a rescue crew on the way to Mars with less than a few hours of prep time.

Arrangements were made, favors were called in, and the E.S.S. Heeren was set to launch two weeks after contact was lost with the Norgay. The Heeren was normally complemented with a crew of three, but five more people were tagging along to aid in the rescue mission. These included two medical personnel, two engineers, and a mission commander from NASA. Luck was on the rescue mission's side, as Mars was almost as close to Earth as it could possibly be right now, and it would take barely a month for the Heeren to reach her.

The mission commander was Colonel Stephanie Welsh, one of NASA's best and brightest. Colonel Welsh had joined the Air Force right after high school, commissioned after a deployment to the Middle East, then rose through the ranks as a natural born pilot and leader. She was all but assured her first General star in the next year or two, and it was no secret she ultimately had her sights set on a Joint Chief position.

The E.S.S. Heeren left the Moon two weeks, one day, four hours, and 42 minutes after all contact was lost with the U.S.S. Tenzing Norgay. During the one-month journey, every available piece of equipment in humanity's space programs was trained towards Mars in an effort to solve what was now one of the biggest mysteries in human history.

Chapter Two

Three weeks into the Heeren's journey, the world was still at a complete loss as to what happened with the Norgay. No new information had been gleaned, and no new signals or transmissions had been picked up. Then, with less than a week before the Heeren was scheduled to arrive at her destination, several very interesting things happened all at once.

First, an Emergency Beacon Probe, or EBP, was mysteriously launched from one of the abandoned outposts on the Martian surface, with a trajectory towards Earth. The EBP was the size of a large shoebox, and was basically the space equivalent of sending up a flare. It consisted of multiple flashing lights and long-distance repeating pulse signals, and had the capability of re-transmitting voice messages over very short distances.

However, it was almost immediately discovered that the lights and pulse signals had been disabled, making the EBP invisible from Earth and useless as an emergency beacon unless a ship was in its immediate vicinity to pick up any possible voice transmissions. In fact, the EBP's launch was only discovered because Earth still had contact with the

Martian Surface Relay System, or MSRS. Compounding the mystery even further, the entire MSRS was completely and inexplicably shut down less than an hour after the EBP's launch.

What this all meant was that an almost completely disabled EBP had been launched from Mars, and the MSRS was left on just long enough for Earth to know about it before everything went dark. Now, the MSRS, the EBP, and of course, the Norgay, were completely out of contact with anyone else in the Solar System.

Since the EBP's last known trajectory was headed towards Earth, this meant that the Heeren would potentially be able to intercept it within the next few days and see if it was transmitting any voice signals. It was still unclear how the EBP had been launched and how the MSRS had been shut down since no one was on the surface of Mars to do it. However, many scientists at NASA, and around the world, surmised it was plausible, though difficult, that the crew of the Norgay was still alive and had somehow hacked the system from orbit to launch the probe before shutting everything down for some reason.

Two days from the Heeren's arrival at Mars, they intercepted the EBP. Rather, they were close enough to its trajectory that they were able to receive the transmission it was broadcasting. The Heeren discovered the EBP's transmission had been artificially weakened, and they were lucky to have intercepted it at all. Just a few hundred kilometers in course change in either the Heeren or EBP and they wouldn't have caught it. The transmission was also very brief, and consisted of a short text, which was almost as cryptic as the Norgay's last message.

The text contained very specific directions for any ship approaching Mars, along with a warning to not attempt travel to the dark side unless flying low-orbit, and shutting down all power save for life support and basic navigational functions. Specifically, total power signature should read less than 20%. The crew of the Heeren quickly realized that due to the size, requirements, and general bulky nature of their ship, it would be impossible to fly into low-orbit or get their power signature below 35%. However, it was discovered that one of the small on-board transport shuttles should be able to make it.

The message contained no information regarding the specific location or condition of either the Norgay or her crew, but the fact that the EBP had been launched at all and contained a message meant that at least one person remained alive, and this glimmer of hope was cause for much rejoicing on Earth.

Strangely, however, the message from the EBP also neglected to address the supposed attack on the Norgay. Since that initial claim almost a month and a half ago, no other ship or probe in the Inner Solar System had reported any sort of attack or unusual phenomenon. India's two probes, now cruising through the Outer Solar System, also failed to detect any odd occurrences save for the brief but suspicious energy surges detected weeks earlier.

The day before the Heeren's arrival to Mars, her course was adjusted to match the instructions given in the message sent by the EBP. This was ultimately determined to involve a bizarre and slightly convoluted approach to the Red Planet, and added another half day to the trip. The E.S.S. Heeren arrived in Martian orbit one month, two days, seven hours, and 58 minutes after launching from the moon.

It was hoped that the Norgay was safe and sound directly on the opposite side of the planet from the Heeren. However, as the Heeren wouldn't be able to make the journey directly, one of her smaller shuttles had to make the trip. Transport Shuttle Tasman was prepped for the short ride to the other side of

Mars. All unnecessary systems were shut down, leaving little more than life support and crucial flight programs operational. The total power signature of the T.S. Tasman was now reading 12%, and her small crew of three prepared for the search for the Norgay.

Colonel Welsh, a medical doctor named F.S. Cummings, and an engineer, Chip Reed, left the docking bay of the Heeren in the Tasman and dropped quickly down into a low-orbit before beginning their flight mere miles above the Martian surface. Welsh, piloting the small craft, was excited for her first Martian flight. In fact, she was the first woman to pilot any craft in the Martian atmosphere, a feat that was celebrated back on Earth, making front-page news everywhere. Four women had already walked on the surface of Mars, but until the T.S. Tasman, all flights to and around the planet had been helmed by men.

After twenty minutes, the Tasman approached the Martian nightfall, and was plunged into total darkness. The only light came from the stars in deep space overhead, and Welsh now had to rely on her instruments to fly. Following the directions from the EBP, Welsh piloted the Tasman along the equator for another twenty minutes, then broke towards the North and began slowing the Tasman while simultaneously increasing her altitude to a much higher orbit.　Fifteen minutes later, a short-range localized pulse beacon began chirping in the Tasman's cockpit.

The U.S.S. Tenzing Norgay had been found.

Chapter Three

The Transport Ship Tasman was now several hundred meters away from the U.S.S. Tenzing Norgay, close enough to see her bulk blotting out the stars overhead. However, she looked completely dead – no lights shone anywhere, and the only indication she was still under any kind of power was the short-range pulse beacon still chirping away in the Tasman's cockpit.

Colonel Welsh slowed the Tasman as more details of the Norgay came into view. She was inverted, with the top of the ship facing towards the planet. This seemed odd to Welsh, as this meant all of the Norgay's cameras and sensory equipment were not facing towards the Martian surface, but rather out into space. Welsh switched on the short-range analog radio of Tasman. Although technically obsolete and outdated equipment, most space craft carried analog radio equipment for emergencies exactly like this one. It consumed almost no power and could universally communicate with every space craft now being operated by humans.

"U.S.S. Tenzing Norgay, this is Colonel Welsh on Transport Shuttle Tasman of the E.S.S. Heeren, over." The signal was layered with static, but still intelligible. Several seconds later, Welsh repeated her message, and then was greeted with a response.

"Colonel Welsh, this is Lieutenant Reyez of the U.S.S. Tenzing Norgay. Good to hear your voice. Over."

Welsh looked over at Reed and Dr. Cummings, and they all shared a smile. "Good to hear yours, too, Lieutenant. Is anyone in need of medical assistance? Over."

"Um... not immediately, Colonel." Welsh shared a confused look with Dr. Cummings, and Lt. Reyez continued. "We're mostly fine. The ship is operational. It would be easier to explain if you just came over. I'm transmitting a docking signal. Lock your ship onto it and we'll guide you to the airlock. Over."

"Roger Wilco. Out."

The Tasman began picking up an automated transmission from the Norgay, and Welsh locked onto it. The Tasman immediately began guiding itself closer to the Norgay, then turned upside down and backwards before finally mating with the Norgay's airlock at the rear of the ship. Lt. Reyez came back over the radio.

"Better get your snow pants on, Colonel. It's gonna be sub-arctic 'til you get to the flight deck. Out."

Welsh turned to her crew mates.

"You two wait here until I figure out what the hell is going on." Reed and Dr. Cummings agreed and Welsh opened a cargo hatch to remove a cold weather suit. The Tasman was small; basically just the cockpit, a 10x15 foot storage room, and an airlock at the rear.

Welsh walked through the storage room to the airlock and unlatched the heavy door. On the other side was the closet-sized airlock chamber of the Tasman, and through the window of the main airlock door, Welsh could see into the airlock chamber of the Norgay. A man dressed in heavy winter clothes was entering the airlock on the other side. He went through the procedure to unlatch the door, finally allowing passage between the two ships.

"Welcome to the Norgay, Colonel. I'm Captain Vanguard. If you'll follow me to the bridge, we'll meet the rest of the crew." Colonel Welsh had studied up on the crew of the Norgay on her journey to Mars. Captain Lance Vanguard was the second-in-command of the ship. He had actually been a professional football player for two seasons before becoming joining the military and eventually becoming an astronaut. He was tall, almost 6'4", and in his heavy winter clothing he almost looked like a giant. Welsh wondered how he was able to cope with the often-cramped quarters of most space craft.

Lt. Costa Reyez was the co-pilot and military engineer of the Norgay. This was his first foray to Mars and one of his first trips into space, period. Dr. Bill Chen was one of the civilian mission specialists; an astro-geographer brought along to study the Martian surface. The other mission specialist was Hank Swanson, an imagery specialist whose job was to maintain the sensors and camera equipment on the Norgay.

Commanding the whole ship was Lieutenant Colonel Jim Westwood. He was the only member of the crew to have been on the surface of Mars before, and, like Welsh, he was a lifelong Airman and natural pilot and leader. Rumor had it his eye was on politics after the completion of this mission.

Welsh followed Vanguard down a series of hallways and up two narrow metal staircases. The ship was dark; the only light coming from tiny, low-wattage, emergency light bulbs interspersed every 20 feet or so. Vanguard explained to her how they were able to get the power signature of the Norgay down to 15%, all without sacrificing life support, artificial gravity, and crucial ship functions. He didn't explain *why* they were doing all that in the first place, nor did he explain why they couldn't just leave if the ship was operational. Welsh figured Lt. Col. Westwood would be explaining all of that.

Vanguard and Welsh arrived at the bridge, where the crew had erected an emergency airlock tent outside the bridge door. Vanguard explained the tent was simply to help keep the heat in and the frigid air out. Inside the tent, Vanguard began to remove his winter clothes and hang them on makeshift hooks next to other sets of winter clothes. Welsh followed suit, but was surprised to see Vanguard continue to remove his flight suit and shirt until he was stripped down to nothing but a pair of athletic shorts. He even kicked off his boots and slipped into a pair of flip-flops. He turned to Welsh and pointed at her flight jacket.

"Uh, you probably won't need that in here, Colonel. It's a little toasty right now."

Welsh removed her jacket and hung it on a hook. The emergency airlock was warmer than the rest of the ship but still fairly cold, and she rubbed some warmth into her bare arms while Vanguard punched in the code to open the bridge door.

Welsh was belted with a burst of dry, hot air as the bridge door opened, and she followed Vanguard inside the darkened bridge.

"Colonel on the bridge!" Vanguard belted as he snapped to attention. The only light on the bridge was coming from lighted knobs, switches, and screens on various control panels, and some starlight from outside the bridge windows. Welsh could see the dark, curving surface of Mars above them, and three other people on the bridge besides Vanguard standing at attention.

"At ease, gentlemen." The crew relaxed, and one of the men approached her from a darkened corner. He extended his hand, and Welsh shook it.

"Colonel Welsh, I'm Lieutenant Colonel Westwood. You've already met Captain Vanguard, Lt. Reyez over here spoke to you on the radio, and this is our astro-geologist, Dr. Chen."

"Good to see you, Colonel."

Welsh took a look around the bridge. Despite the darkness, she could see some bedding and pillows piled up in a corner, as well as multiple boxes of rations, several stacks of books, and what seemed to be an almost full trash can. It looked like the crew had been living on the bridge.

"Colonel, have you and your crew been living on the bridge?"

"Yes, Ma'am," he replied. "We've had to shut down almost all environmental control systems to the rest of the ship to stay at 15%, which is why it's like a meat locker out there. Unfortunately, that means the circulation system isn't quite up to speed, which is also why it's so hot in here. We've been fine tuning things, though. A couple weeks ago it was a good five degrees hotter."

As her eyes continued to adjust to the darkness, Welsh could see that all four men were indeed shirtless, wearing nothing but gym shorts and flip-flips. She might have to join them if she was going to stay on the bridge much longer.

Vanguard joined Dr. Chen at a computer console, and they began poring over the screen. Reyez was on the other side of the bridge rummaging through a ration box. Westwood turn to Vanguard and Chen.

"Any movement?" he said.

"No, sir," Dr. Chen said. "Nothing. I think we're clear."

"Good," Westwood turned back to Welsh. "We were wondering if your arrival was going to alert the neighbors, but it looks like you followed our instructions to the tee."

"Colonel Westwood, what the hell is going on out here? You've had the whole of humanity obsessing over this ship for the last month and a half."

Reyez looked up from the pile of rations and said, "Shut the fuck up. Seriously?"

"Costa…" Westwood said, using Reyez's first name in a scolding tone.

"Sorry, sir."

Welsh spoke. "Seriously. The President of the United States has visited all of your families in person. People are already talking about naming schools after you."

Now Dr. Chen chimed in. "The Dr. Bill Chen School for the Economically Disadvantaged. What do you think, fellas?"

Vanguard slapped him a high five and responded, "That's what I'm talkin' about."

"Okay, boys, that's enough," Westwood guided Welsh over to the terminal where Vanguard and Chen were posted. "You'll have to excuse us, ma'am. We've been dealing with a little cabin fever in here. Okay, now let me explain. About six weeks ago, everything was fine, we were mapping the surface, doing what we came out here to do. Then, as we said in our last transmission, we were attacked."

"*Who* attacked you?" Welsh was dying to know. Billions of people were dying to know.

"Aliens," Westwood answered without any hesitation.

Welsh had a sudden fear that the crew had all gone crazy, shut down their ship for no reason, driven the whole world mad, and brought the Heeren out on a wild goose chase.

"Aliens," she repeated.

"Yes, ma'am. Aliens. We were scanning the surface, right about where we are now, on the dark side of Mars, when a projectile rocketed within several hundred meters of our position. It flew around trying to hit us, we assume, before exploding in orbit. Dr. Chen, play the footage."

Westwood directed Welsh's attention to the computer screen, and he continued speaking. "This is footage from six weeks ago. Watch the right side of the screen."

Welsh leaned closer to the monitor. It was initially a black screen, but Dr. Chen began dialing in the brightness and resolution to reveal a night-vision image of the Martian surface. Nothing happened for a few seconds, then a ball of light appeared on the right side of the screen and began hurtling towards the planet. About halfway down, it abruptly changed course, corkscrewed around for a few seconds, then shot off the left side of the screen. There was a bright flash as if the ball exploded, and then nothing.

"That was no meteor," said Westwood. "We ran it through every scanner we have, which, as you know, is all state-of-the-art. That projectile was artificially constructed. And whatever it was, it was traveling at near light-speed before slowing down. We just happen to be stargazing out of the bridge windows here, and saw it coming in from the direction of the Main Belt before it came into camera view. Now, look at this. Chen?" Dr. Chen began pulling up some more footage.

"After that happened, we decided to turn the ship around to point the cameras and sensory equipment out into space, to see if we could see anything. At first, nothing... but when we played the footage back at different wavelengths, we saw this..."

The screen showed a black field of stars, then Dr. Chen hit a switch. The view switched to a different wavelength, and a small point of light immediately stood out to Welsh. It was colored a bright red, and creeping diagonally across the center of the screen.

"It's moving away from us, towards the Main Belt, ten times faster than anything we have."

The red light took up a position within the Main Asteroid Belt and then stopped. It dimmed to about 50% of its original brigtness.

Westwood pointed over to another computer screen in the center of the bridge.

"That's a live feed. That red light is still there, in the Main Asteroid Belt, tracking Mars' revolution around the Sun."

Welsh cautiously spoke up. "So, you think that's an alien ship, that fired on the Norgay, and then retreated into the Belt? And now it's watching you?"

Westwood continued. "Yes. When they dimmed, we figured they were trying to hide from our sensors, so we decided to do the same, and shut everything down. Maybe let them think they destroyed us or something. At least not give them anything to lock on to for another shot."

"So why didn't you just leave orbit and head back to Earth?" asked Welsh.

"That was our plan," explained Westwood. "To just slip out of orbit on minimal power. But then we calculated that, even as far away as the Alien ship was, if we were running at anything over 25%, they would be able to spot us and fire on us before we could even get up to speed. The Norgay is basically dead weight at anything under 30%. We've been operating at sub-20, just to be safe, and that's what we put in our EBP message."

"How did you manage to launch it?" asked Welsh.

Vanguard took this one. "We've had a lot of spare time on our hands. Dr. Chen wrote a few programs and was able to hack into the MSRS. We uploaded a brief message into an EBP, launched it to run on minimal power, and then shut the whole system down to get y'all's attention. Looks like it worked."

"We were just days away when we intercepted the EBP," Welsh admitted. Then something caught her eye. The Norgay had a crew complement of five. Yet she had only seen four people on board so far, and the bridge was supposedly the only inhabitable place on the ship.

"Colonel," Welsh said as she paced around the cramped bridge. "Where's the fifth crew member? The imagery specialist. Swanson was his name, I believe?"

The four present members of the Norgay crew froze and looked at each other. Westwood spoke up.

"Hank Swanson… we've hit a bit of a snag with him. He seems to have had somewhat of a mental break."

"What do you mean?" Welsh inquired.

Chen replied, "He went crazy. We take shifts at night watching the Alien ship to see if it moves. He kept thinking he could hear voices whenever he was on watch. He said he was able to tune his equipment in to catch their communications. But that's impossible… that ship is too far away for us to pick up anything like that, especially running on low power."

Reyez added, "He kept trying to show us how it worked, but he could never pick up the signal with other people listening. He finally snapped, started running around the ship in the freezing cold, looking for aliens in the ceiling and floor and everywhere else."

"Where is he now?" Welsh was afraid of the answer she might get.

"We managed to subdue him and lock him in the gym," Westwood responded.

"Why there?"

"The Engine Thermal Vents run underneath the floor of the gym and then up the walls on both sides. Normally, when we're running at regular power, we have to artificially cool the room, otherwise it would get too hot. Now, even in a low power state, the engines are providing enough heat to keep the gym at a steady 68 degrees. It's the only room on the ship we don't have to waste power keeping warm, so we threw him in there."

"Oh, my god…" Welsh was having trouble taking all of this in. "How long has he been in there?"

"Just a couple weeks," Reyes said. "I've been taking care of him. We bring him food and books. He seems to have calmed down some, but still goes on about the voices every once in a while, and generally acts kind of sketchy. Other than that, he just reads and works out all day."

Welsh used her jacket to dab the sweat off of her face. "Well, we're going to get you guys out of here. I've got a doctor on the Tasman. We can have him take a look at Swanson."

Just then, the analog radio crackled to life. "Colonel Welsh, this is Reed. Over."

Reyez picked up the handset and held it out to Welsh. She walked over to him and took it. "Reed, this is Welsh, over."

There was some hesitation before the engineer on the Tasman responded. "Colonel, uh… for the last five minutes we've been hearing voices on one of the analog radio channels."

Chapter Four

Colonel Welsh and the crew of the Norgay all looked around at each other in astonishment. Lieutenant Reyez finally hopped into action and began fiddling with knobs and switches at a computer terminal off to the left side of the bridge.

"Why the hell haven't *we* been hearing anything?" demanded Lieutenant Colonel Westwood.

"I don't know, sir," answered Reyez. "Technically, very few analog frequencies are currently in use by the world's space programs. Frequencies that aren't being used are basically 'turned off' on each ship, otherwise we'd just constantly be scanning dead air for no reason. If the voices are coming across one of those channels, then we wouldn't be hearing it."

Welsh spoke into the analog handset. "Reed, this is Welsh. What frequency are you hearing the voices on? Over."

"Seven-seven-niner-point-one. Over." Reyez immediately began tuning in to 779.1.

Welsh turned to Westwood and said, "When we were readying the Tasman for the flight out here, we shut down the systems that weren't vital, and then did a complete reboot of what was left. The analog radio uses so little power we didn't even pay attention to it. It's possible that rebooting it opened up the entire range of frequencies for us to hear."

Dr. Chen had a sudden realization. "So... Hank wasn't crazy after all. He *was* hearing voices. But how?"

Captain Vanguard decided to hazard a guess, and said, "He was constantly messing with his imaging and scanning equipment on night watch. He probably just happened across those dead frequencies somehow when they were transmitting."

Reyez finally had the radio tuned in to what the Tasman had been hearing, and he flipped on the sound so the whole crew could hear through the speakers on the bridge. The voices were barely discernable through a heavy layer of static, but they were definitely organic, and not anything mechanical or naturally occurring. Individual words or sounds could not really be distinguished, but there was a clearly discernable sing-song quality of speech present, and occasional whistles and pops could be heard. It was not human.

Westwood began to think things through. "If this is analog, then whatever is transmitting that is really close. It's not us, it's not the Tasman, we've completely shut down the Martian Surface Relay System…"

"And Mars is blocking any signals between the Norgay and the Heeren," Welsh added.

"Yes," Westwood continued. He looked over at the computer screen of the live feed of the so-called alien ship. The bright red dot was still sitting there, motionless. "Wherever that signal is coming from, it's within a few hundred kilometers of us right now."

Vanguard moved over to a terminal and tapped a few keys on a keyboard. "Scanners are picking up nothing. Except for the Heeren, we're alone out here for millions of miles in any direction."

"Wait a minute…" Reyez jumped in. "Nothing?"

Vanguard looked at the terminal again. "Nope. Nothing."

"That can't be right. You should at least be picking up two or three of the MSRS relay antennas on the surface. Even if they're shut down. They should still pop up on the resonance scan."

Vanguard looked back down at the terminal and hit a few more keys. "What the hell… it's like they're not even there," he said as he looked up at Westwood.

Westwood thought a moment and then said to Reyez, "Increase power to the scanners by... 15%."

Reyez adjusted some knobs and dipswitches on a different terminal, then looked over to Vanguard, who looked down at the scanner terminal.

"Still nothing," he said.

"Increase another 15%," ordered Westwood. Reyez did so, and several blips appeared on Vanguard's terminal.

"There!" he exclaimed, and pointed at his screen. "Relay antennas just popped up. Those antennas are barely bigger than a person. They were probably too small to get picked up by the scanners on such a low power threshold."

"Reyez," said Westwood cautiously. "Turn the scanners up as far as they'll go without taking our total power signature over 20%."

"Yes, sir," Reyez complied.

Another blip suddenly appeared on Vanguard's terminal. "Sir!" he said.

Westwood and Welsh crowded around him and looked down at the screen. Vanguard spoke, "There's something in orbit, less than 300 kilometers away from us, and matching our trajectory and speed almost exactly."

"Is that where the transmissions are coming from?" asked Welsh.

Vanguard adjusted a knob, and a confused look spread across his face. "I'm not getting any kind of power readings or anything. Hang on a second..." He sat down in front of the terminal and entered some commands on the keyboard. "There!" He pointed to the main screen of the bridge.

A black-and-white, artificial, pixelated image appeared line-by-line on the monitor. It was a crude picture that was reminiscent of something that would have been printed by a dot matrix printer from decades ago. Still, the image was clear enough that many details could be made out. The crew looked in amazement at what appeared to be an elongated egg shape, with about a third of the end blown out and ending in jagged points. About twenty or thirty thick cables seemed to emanate from this end and were lazily twisting in all directions.

"What the hell is that?" asked Reyez.

Westwood walked up to the screen to get a closer look. "It looks like a big squid."

Vanguard shook his head and said, "It's definitely constructed. It's not natural or organic in any way. I'm not getting any kind of signals or readings from it. Whatever it is, it's totally dead in the water."

"It's the remains of whatever that alien ship shot at us. It has to be," postulated Reyez. "Maybe that's why they're still hanging out in the Main Belt… they've been trying to make contact with it this whole time."

"Vanguard… you're not picking up any life readings?"

Vanguard spent a few seconds looking at a readout on the terminal. "Negative, sir. It's cold as ice."

"Okay…" Westwood took some deep breaths. "Here's what we're gonna do. Dr. Chen, go get Swanson. Reyez, download all the data you can on everything we've seen and done up to five seconds ago. We're getting out of here. We'll take the Tasman on a flyby of the wreckage to see if we can see anything, then we'll high-tail it back to the Heeren. From there we'll transmit everything back to Earth and let them worry about this. We're not equipped to deal with alien encounters in any way." Westwood turned to Welsh and said, "Sound good, Ma'am?" Welsh nodded her head.

Chen walked from his computer terminal to the bridge door and opened it to enter the emergency airlock. Welsh felt a deliciously cool breeze waft into the room, and then addressed Westwood.

"What do you need from me?"

"We need to start loading our personal gear and sensitive equipment onto the Tasman. Tell your guys to stand by the airlock and get ready to help."

In the emergency airlock, Chen finished up putting on his winter gear, and headed through the ship to gym, which was on Deck Two, almost in the direct center of the Norgay. The gym was about ten by twenty feet in size and contained a treadmill, some pullup bars, an adjustable dumbbell and barbell set, and other fitness related accessories. The door to the gym was on one of the shorter sides of the room, facing the rear of the ship.

Chen looked into the round window of the gym door, but didn't see Hank Swanson anywhere. Chen assumed that Hank was in the bathroom at the rear of the gym, so he entered an access code and the heavy door to the gym slid open. It was a good 80 degrees warmer in here than the frigid hallways of the rest of the ship, so Chen stepped inside, shut the door behind him, and removed his heavy parka. He dropped it onto the cot that the crew had set up for Hank near the entrance and looked around.

As usual, the weights and some other equipment was scattered around the room; Swanson had little else to do in this small room but workout. There were quite a few stacks of books underneath the cot, and the remnants of a military issue Meal, Ready-to Eat on top of the cot. Chen reached down to touch the heating packet included with every MRE and discovered it was quite warm, indicating very recent use.

Chen walked to the back of the gym to knock on the bathroom door.

"Hank, you in there, buddy? It's Bill."

There was no answer.

"Hey, you're not gonna believe this, but you were right about those voices. We finally picked up a transmission that we think —"

Chen stopped talking when he realized the "Occupied" light on the bathroom door was not lit up. He pushed the open button and the door quietly slid sideways into the wall, revealing an empty bathroom.

Chen whipped around. There was nowhere in the gym to hide. It was just a big, bare room with a few pieces of gym equipment in it. He looked back into the empty bathroom again, just to make sure he wasn't going crazy, and then ran to the front of the gym. Chen grabbed his parka, and paused, looking down at the cot. He grabbed it with one hand and flipped it over. A few stacks of books toppled over, but no one was hiding underneath.

"Shit, shit, shit…" he repeated as he began buttoning up his coat. He threw open the gym door and ran out into the arctic chill of the ship. The onboard ship communications had been shut down to reduce power, so there was no way to notify the rest of the crew that Hank Swanson was now missing. Chen was closer to the airlock than the bridge, so he ran down another level and towards the rear of the ship to see if anyone was there.

Vanguard and Welsh had just arrived at the airlock in their heavy winter clothes, each awkwardly carrying several metal cases of equipment. Vanguard was in the process of opening the airlock door to greet the crew of the Tasman on the other side just as Chen ran up to them.

"Hank's gone. He's not in the gym," he said, breathing heavily.

Vanguard looked at Welsh and then back to Chen. "How's that possible?"

"I don't know… the door was locked. He just wasn't in there."

"Shit…" Vanguard paused. "Help Colonel Welsh load this stuff in. I'll run and tell the Captain."

Just as he finished his sentence, several loud metallic clangs could be heard reverberating through the ship, followed by a low humming.

"What is that?" asked Welsh.

Overhead lights began flickering to life up and down the hallway, and a rush of warm air could be felt emanating from the air vents.

Vanguard said, "The ship is powering up." He exchanged a worried look with Chen and then took off running toward the bridge.

Chapter Five

Captain Vanguard literally ripped through the outer sheet of the emergency airlock tent and pounded the buttons to open the bridge door. All of the lights were on; he hadn't seen it so bright in here in weeks, and it looked like a homeless shelter stocked with computers. Lieutenant Colonel Westwood was frantically bouncing around between three computer terminals, flipping switches off and on, entering commands on keyboards, and pounding the tops of monitors. Lieutenant Reyez was trying to coil up some cables when he looked over at Vanguard.

"What the fuck is happening?" Reyez blurted out. "Why is the ship turning back on?"

"It's Swanson. He's escaped. I think he's turning on the ship somehow."

"Yeah, well, he's fucked us... look!" Reyez pointed to the computer screen that had the constant live feed of the alien ship's position in the Main Belt. It was gone. There was no tiny red light in the center of the screen anymore.

"Where did they go?" asked Vanguard.

Westwood answered without looking up from a terminal. "As soon as the power started coming on, I looked over at the screen. I saw them take off like a bat out of hell. They must be going near light-speed. We need to get out of here, now! They could be on us in seconds."

Reyez grabbed an armload of hard drives and cables, and took off running through the bridge door, still in his shorts and flip-flops. The environmental systems were back online and blowing hot air so there was no need for heavy winter clothes anymore.

"Reyez, wait!" shouted Westwood, and Reyez stuck his head back in the room.

"Sir?"

"Give that shit to Vanguard. I need you to start burning everything you haven't already downloaded. We'll leave the Norgay here as a decoy and try to escape on the Tasman. We can't leave anything vital for them to find."

Vanguard ran over to Reyez and took the load before running off the bridge. Reyez went back over to his main work station and cracked his knuckles.

"Delete everything, sir?"

"Reyez, I even want you to delete the code that flushes the toilets."

"Yes, sir."

Westwood walked over to the front of the bridge, picked up a handset, and spoke into it. Now that the ship was on the communications systems were working. His voice boomed through the entire ship.

"Swanson? Can you hear me? Swanson. If you can hear me, pick up a handset and answer. This is Colonel Westwood."

Westwood waited a good twenty seconds but there was no response. He threw down the handset with a huff and grabbed a duffel bag from the corner.

"When you're done with that," he said to Reyez, "grab your stuff and head to the airlock."

"Yes, sir."

Colonel Welsh, Dr. Chen, and now Vanguard were down at the airlock handing off another load of equipment over to Dr. Cummings and Reed on the Tasman.

"This is all the important stuff," explained Vanguard as they loaded the last box. "Everything else is disposable."

"Where's the Lieutenant and Captain?" asked Welsh.

Just then, Westwood appeared at the end of the hallway, trotting towards the airlock. "Right here," he said. "Reyez is right behind me. Is everything loaded up?"

"Yes, sir," answered Vanguard. "Soon as Reyez gets here we can leave. Still no sign of Swanson."

Westwood threw his duffel bag through the airlock into the Tasman. "I have no idea what he did, or how he did it. I tried to shut the power back down from the bridge, but nothing worked."

Just then, the entire ship went completely dead, and the crew was enveloped in pitch blackness. The background humming of the engines ceased, and the air vents went silent.

"Shit. Now what?" It was Chen who spoke.

Several beams of light appeared from the Tasman, and Cummings and Reed appeared with flashlights.

"Ma'am…" Cummings shone his light at Welsh's waist. "We've just picked up a ship on the scanner. It appeared out of nowhere. They've stopped about 500 kilometers from us. It's not one of ours. Doesn't match records of anything from Earth."

A shout was heard from the end of the hallway, and another flashlight beam appeared running towards the airlock. It was Reyez.

"Sorry! That was me. I forgot to put a delay on the lights and air when I deleted everything. But we have about four minutes before the artificial gravity shuts down."

"Did you happen to see Swanson?" asked Chen.

"Negative. I ran by the gym again, just in case, but he wasn't there."

"Okay, everyone on the Tasman," ordered Westwood. "If I'm not back by the time the gravity shuts off, leave without me. If the alien ship comes any closer, leave without me."

Welsh, Chen, and Reyez boarded the Tasman and Vanguard stood guard by the airlock door. Westwood kicked off his flip-flops and took off running barefoot down the hallway, and started shouting Swanson's name. He ran up to Deck Two, made a lap by the gym, and then headed up towards the bridge. The door was open, and he shone his flashlight around inside.

Swanson was standing at the front of the bridge, staring out of the large bay windows, a mylar emergency blanket wrapped around him. In the distance, the alien ship could be seen, floating through space. It was absolutely massive. Despite being 500 kilometers away, Westwood could see details such as protruding pylons and multiple colored lights running up and down the whole ship.

"Hank…" Westwood uttered calmly.

Swanson turned around. He was crying.

"I'm sorry… I'm so sorry… what have I done?"

"Hank, we're getting out of here. Now. Come on." We only have a minute or two. Westwood walked towards Swanson and held out his hand. Swanson hesitated a second and then took it.

"Come on, let's go."

Down at the airlock, Vanguard was shining his light up and down the hallway, craning his neck to listen for noises of anyone approaching. Suddenly, he felt a tingle in his legs, which then crept up his whole body, followed by an odd sensation in his stomach.

He turned to shout into the Tasman, "Gravity's shutting down. Get ready." He turned and shone his light back down the hallway, and was shocked to see Westwood and Swanson bounding towards him, their steps covering 20 feet at a time in the low gravity. They were at the airlock in seconds.

"Let's go," said Westwood, and they piled into the Tasman, manually shutting the airlock door behind them. The Tasman detached from the Norgay and dropped down into a low-orbit, moving as fast as her low power state would allow. For as long as the

Tasman was able to track the alien ship, she never made a move towards either the Tasman or the Norgay.

Welsh brought the Tasman back into the daylight, and within minutes they were safe and sound back on board the Heeren. The crew of the Norgay was immediately given full medical scans, and the Heeren left Martian orbit and began the month-long journey back to Earth.

The crews of the Norgay and Heeren were given heroes' welcomes upon their return, and scientists began poring over the information brought back regarding both the Martian surface and the alien ship. Although the Norgay hadn't technically finished her mission, NASA had enough information to locate a suitable location for a permanent settlement on Mars.

Several military space craft had been deployed within days of the Heeren announcing the crew had been rescued, but no trace of the alien ship or orbiting debris was ever found upon their arrival at Mars. The Chinese mining drones eventually made their way to the area of the Main Asteroid Belt where the ship had been hiding out, but nothing was found.

Plans for the permanent Martian settlement were delayed for several years while the powers-that-be debated whether or not the aliens would ever attack again. Based on what the crew of the Norgay had reported, and the data they had brought back, it was decided that the aliens were technologically advanced enough that there was no point in holding off any further. If they really wanted to attack humans, they could be anywhere in the Solar System within minutes.

Lt. Col. Welsh and the crew of the Norgay would spend the rest of their lives never seeing humanity have another alien encounter, and never hearing the alien voices decoded. And, as one final, mysterious piece of the puzzle, the dark, abandoned, lifeless hulk of the U.S.S. Tenzing Norgay was never seen again.

Operator

Chapter One

Trevor Campbell slowly opened his eyes, and looked up at the dark ceiling. Early morning sunlight was creeping in from a heavily curtained window to his left, but it wasn't enough to illuminate any specific details of the room. He turned his head to look around in the dark. He could barely make out a dresser on the far wall, and a nightstand by the bed with a lamp on it.

Odd, he thought, as his eyes began to adjust. There didn't seem to be any hospital equipment in here. He felt around under the thin bedsheet covering his body. He was nude, and couldn't feel any IV tubes or medical sensors attached to his arms or torso. How long had he been out?

The last thing he remembered was an IED going off on the side of the road as his Humvee drove past it. He was standing in the gunner's turret, manning the M249 SAW, while Specialist Bradley drove and Staff Sergeant Moss sat in the passenger seat. They were the second Humvee in a convoy escorting a resupply truck to the Iraqi town of Rabeaa on the Syrian border. Suddenly, a roadside bomb went off, Trevor was knocked unconscious, and then...

115

He was alone in a cold room. The more his eyes adjusted to the dark, the more he could see that this was no hospital room. It looked like someone's bedroom. *His* bedroom? No, this wasn't his... He sat up from the bed and felt around his body again. He could feel no injuries from the blast. His ears weren't ringing, his head didn't hurt...

He reached up to feel his head and realized his hair was a lot longer than it should be. It covered his ears and almost reached the bottom of his neck. Had he been in a coma? He had months of hair growth, if not close to a year. No, he couldn't have been in a coma... people who wake up from comas can barely move, and he actually felt great. Despite having just woken up, he felt neither stiff nor tired.

Trevor pulled the sheet aside and got out of bed. He reached over to turn on the bedside lamp. He was definitely in a bedroom of a residential house. He looked back at the twin bed he had just gotten out of. It *looked* like a hospital bed; the mattress was thin and the frame was welded metal. Over the bed on the wall was a movie poster for Close Encounters of the Third Kind.

He walked around the end of the bed to the lone window of the room. The curtains were thick, heavy, and sewn of an ugly orange and brown material. He opened one side of the curtains and looked out the window. He was looking into a backyard, with a wooden privacy fence running around the perimeter. He could see the roofs of other houses above the top of the fence. The yard was empty, and most of the grass was dead. The few trees he could see were devoid of leaves, and in the corners of the yard up against the fence were small piles of snow. It was winter.

Trevor had definitely been out for a while. It was late August when he was knocked unconscious. Now it was, what… December? February? He didn't know. He also didn't recognize this room, or the backyard. For the first time in the light he glanced down at his body. It was noticeably more muscular than before. And something else was just… off. It was like he was in someone else's body, in someone else's house.

He abruptly turned around, walked to the bedroom door, and opened it. He was looking down a short hallway, with two doors on either side about halfway down. The hallway appeared to end in a living room, and was lit by dim daylight coming in from the sides. Trevor walked down the hall and discovered the door on the left was open and led into an empty bedroom. The door on the right was a bathroom.

He walked into the bathroom, turned on the light, and looked in the mirror. No, he was definitely still Trevor Campbell. He recognized himself in the mirror. But he had changed… his hair was longer, shaggier… he was more muscular, and… he was older. He couldn't tell how much older, but it was distinct, and noticeable. Years. Maybe 10 or 12?

Trevor could see no injuries on his body from an IED blast. He realized again how great he felt. He almost felt like he could walk out into the cold, totally naked, and run five miles. It *was* a little chilly in the house, though… maybe he should just see if he could find some clothes.

He first decided to pee, since he had apparently just had a great night's sleep. As he stood at the toilet, relieving his bladder, Trevor looked around the bathroom and noticed how out of date it was. It looked like it was built in the '60s and never updated. Oh, well, he thought… people are really into retro stuff nowadays.

He turned the light off in the bathroom and went back to the bedroom. He walked over the dresser and opened the top drawer. It was full of socks, underwear, and plain white t-shirts. After putting on one of each, he opened the second drawer. This one

118

was stocked with jeans. He removed a pair and put them on. The third drawer contained several solid color athletic sweaters. He removed a grey one and put it on. The fourth drawer was empty. The clothes all fit him perfectly. These were left here for *him*.

Trevor turned around and walked over to the nightstand. He opened the lone drawer and saw a wristwatch and a brown leather wallet. He picked up the stainless-steel watch and looked at the black dial. It was nice... a high-end Swiss job, worth several thousand dollars. The hands were both pointing at 12, and the watch was not running. Trevor unscrewed the crown and gave it a full wind to get it going before putting it on his wrist. He would have to remember to set it when he actually figured out what time it was.

He next reached into the drawer to remove the wallet. It was worn in spots, but still in good shape. He opened it. On the left side was a clear window, holding a driver license. The license was for Trevor Campbell, but it was strange-looking. It looked cheap and handmade, with the information looking like it was typed on a typewriter. Trevor's picture looked much like he did now, with an aged look and shaggy hair.

Then he looked at the information again. Minnesota. The expiration date read

119

12/28/1980. His date of birth? 4/2/1940. What the hell? Why did he have a fake Minnesota driver license that expired decades ago? The other side of the wallet held several credit cards. Trevor removed these and looked at them. They looked vintage, and had similar expiration dates to the license. He put them back in their respective slots and opened up the main pouch of the wallet.

It was full of hundred-dollar bills. Maybe 20 of them, all crisp and brand new. There was also a business card for a local bank, and when Trevor turned the card over, he saw a number hand written on it. An account number, perhaps?

He closed the wallet and stuck it in his pocket. There didn't seem to be anything else to look at in the room so he decided to explore the rest of the house. The other bedroom was completely empty. Trevor discovered some basic grooming supplies in a bathroom drawer; toothbrush, toothpaste, comb, electric razor, some dental floss... In the shower was a brand-new bottle of shampoo and a wrapped bar of soap. A clean towel was hanging on the towel rack. Trevor suddenly realized he didn't feel "dirty" like he normally does after waking up in the morning. He didn't smell and his hair felt quite clean and fluffy.

At the end of the hallway was a large room that functioned as a living room and dining room. On the living room side, to the right, was a large bay window and the front door of the house. There was a matching couch and recliner, both covered with hideous brown and tan fabric and positioned around a coffee table. A massive cabinet television set sat on the floor across from the couch.

The dining room side, to the left, held a round wooden table, surrounded by four matching wooden chairs. A sliding glass door led out to the back yard. Continuing on through this room, Trevor headed into the kitchen. On the kitchen counter was an unopened box of toaster pastries with a hand-written note taped to it. The note read:

"Sorry, didn't have time to get food... this will tide you over until you can get to the store. There's milk in the fridge."

Trevor examined the box of toaster pastries. It looked vintage yet brand new at the same time. He opened the refrigerator and discovered a quart of milk on the top shelf. Nothing else was in the refrigerator, but the freezer held three full trays of ice cubes.

The cabinets of the kitchen were empty except for a basic set of dishes. Trevor removed a drinking glass and filled it with milk. He couldn't actually find a toaster anywhere in the kitchen, so he just grabbed the box of pastries and headed over to the couch. He didn't see a TV remote, so he put the milk and pastries down on the table, walked over to the TV, and turned it on. A news program immediate came to life.

As Trevor sat on the couch eating cold, unfrosted, strawberry filled toaster pastries and drinking Vitamin D milk, he was mesmerized by a local Minnesota morning news broadcast that claimed it was shortly after 7am on Wednesday, January 4th, 1978. He watched in amazement for about 15 minutes, then got up to check the TV, looking for some sort of VCR or other input. The only cables coming from the TV went to the electrical outlet and the rabbit ear antenna on top. Trevor fiddled with the antenna and the screen briefly wobbled with static.

He didn't know what to do with this information. The news, the retro house, the old looking ID cards... somebody really wanted him to think he was in Minnesota in the year 1978. And his hair and body... he had definitely changed as well. He was no longer the young Infantryman Specialist cruising through Iraq in the Summer of 2003. He thought again of the birth date on his driver license – April, 1940. If this was January, 1978, that would make him about 37

122

years old. He certainly looked it. He had somehow aged 12 years from being knocked out in Iraq and then, on top of that, sent back in time 25 years.

And yet… somebody was trying to *help* him for some reason. They apologized for not having enough food, and gave him a wallet with $2,000 in it and a wristwatch worth more than that. That's right, the watch… he took it off his wrist and set it to the time displayed on the news.

By the time the news program was over, Trevor had eaten four pastries and drank two glasses of milk. He went to the restroom and brushed his teeth. Upon walking back out in the hallway, he remembered a door in the kitchen that he hadn't opened yet.

He walked over to it and opened it. It led to a garage housing a washer, a dryer, and a boxy, four-door, brown sedan. Immediately to Trevor's left, level to his head, was a set of car keys hanging from a hook on the wall. The garage was otherwise empty, but several shelves stood empty along the length of two walls.

There was no phone in the house to try and call anyone. Trevor wasn't sure what else to do around the house, so he decided to go for a drive to see what else was around the neighborhood. He walked through the garage to the garage door and manually opened it. He was immediately hit with a burst of frigid winter air.

"Holy shit," he exclaimed out loud, before thinking it must be well below freezing. He was definitely in Minnesota in the wintertime.

Trevor turned around and walked back into the house. In the living room he had seen a narrow door which he had assumed was a closet. Upon opening the door, he discovered several coats and jackets, a few pairs of sneakers, and some boots. He selected a pair of plain white sneakers and the heaviest coat, a black parka with a fur lined hood. He was pleased to find some leather gloves in the pockets, as well.

Wait a minute… he thought. Where were the house keys? He hadn't yet found any in his search of the house. He donned the coat and walked back out to the garage. Examining the keys hanging on the wall, he did indeed discover an additional set of keys not belonging to the car. He spent the next couple of minutes testing the keys, and found out they unlocked the front door, the sliding door in the dining room, and the manual garage door. There was also a smaller key on the ring that didn't seem to fit any locks in the house.

Trevor made sure everything was locked up and got in the car, pulling it out into the driveway. The tank was full, and it seemed to be running smoothly. Before getting in the car, he noticed the tires were brand new. He got out of the car and closed the garage door. He also made a mental note of the house number; 3216.

The house Trevor had woken up in was near the end of a cul-de-sac, so there was only one way to go. Driving to the end of the street, Trevor looked left and saw more houses. To the right, one block down, he could see a main road with cars driving back and forth. He turned right and headed down to the intersection.

Trevor looked right and saw more subdivision. To the left, he could immediately see this was where he wanted to head; about a half-mile down there were multiple commercial buildings and signs advertising businesses and restaurants. Not a single car that he could see on the road looked like it was made after 1980. Trevor could even see some cars from the '50s and '60s driving around.

He waited for a break in the traffic and turned left. In less than a minute he was driving through a shopping district. One of the first businesses to his right was a large grocery store. Remembering the stranger's note about not having time to buy food, Trevor figured he should probably take care of that right now. He really wasn't sure what else he could be doing, anyway.

He parked towards the back of the lot and walked into the store, grabbing a shopping cart on the way in. He was absolutely amazed at what he saw. The inside of the store looked like a food museum. In fact, it looked like a museum, period. Everything from the overhead lights, the checkout lanes, the shelves, the clothes the people were wearing... Trevor was a baby when things still looked like this.

Not wanting to appear oblivious, he immediately made his way down the first aisle of the store. Trevor once read a book on spy craft, and one of the first rules you learn is to pretend like you belong, no matter where you are. This simple act will allay 90% of the suspicion people will have about you.

Trevor had almost gotten to the end of the first aisle when he realized he already passed by several things he needed. He was just so enthralled by looking at what he would refer to as vintage and retro packaging design that he forgot to put things in his cart. He turned around and went back down the aisle.

By the end of the shopping trip, Trevor had a good two weeks' worth of food in his cart. He figured that would be plenty for now, even if the mysterious note writer ever showed back up to the house and he had to share some food. He also picked up two different newspapers and several magazines covering topical subjects and entertainment gossip. If he was going to be living in the late 1970's, he should probably be up on current events. He knew Jimmy Carter would be President right now, and there was an oil crisis at some point (was it over yet? There seemed to be a lot of cars on the road...), but otherwise he was basically clueless about this point in history.

Trevor was pretty much convinced now that he had somehow traveled back in time to 1978, as ridiculous as that sounded. It wouldn't be *too* hard to fake a house and the few items laying around it to appear as such, but to fake an entire grocery store, with fully stocked shelves, accurate to the last detail, and dozens of vintage cars on the road... that was something else altogether.

Out in the parking lot, as Trevor was loading the groceries in the trunk of his car, he looked up and saw a bank on the other side of the parking lot. The business card in his wallet was from the same bank. He decided to drive home, unload the groceries, and then come back to inquire about the information written on the back of the card.

About 15 minutes later he was back at the bank and sitting in a parking spot right outside the front door. He was looking at the business card from his wallet and making sure the number written on the back was legible. After unloading his groceries, he had compared the writing on the card with the note from the kitchen, and from what he could tell they appeared to have been written by the same hand, probably even with the same blue pen. He got out of the car and walked into the bank.

There was no one in line so he walked right up to the first teller, a young blond woman, maybe in her mid-20's. Trevor simply handed her the business card and his driver license and asked for a total balance on the account. The woman entered the number on what appeared to Trevor to be an ancient computer. Her mouth opened as if to say something, but then she turned away from Trevor and picked up a phone on a desk behind her. She spoke for a second and then hung up the phone.

"Is everything okay?" asked Trevor.

"Yes, sir. Mr. Cornwall will be helping you," she said as she handed Trever the business card and his license.

At that moment, a balding, middle-aged man in a suit appeared behind Trevor. He smiled and extended his hand. Trevor shook it.

"Mr. Campbell? I'm Roger Cornwall. Won't you step into my office, please?" He gestured towards an open door to the side of the lobby, and led Trevor to it as he spoke.

"Your associate came in last week to set up the account and said you would be by to finish up the paperwork."

"My associate…" mumbled Trevor. He wanted to ask who his associate supposedly was, but he also didn't want to be obvious about it. He thought of a quick ruse, and asked, "Oh, was it Jerry Seinfeld?"

"No, sir," Mr. Cornwall said as he sat down behind a desk in his office. He picked up a piece of paper and said, "A Mr… Ike Wallbauer."

Trevor sat down in a leather-bound chair across from Mr. Cornwall.

"Ah! Ike. Indeed. Good man, good man." Trevor continued the ruse. He had never heard the name Ike Wallbauer before in his life. Was it an alias for someone he *did* know? Was it the man who had been leaving Trevor notes back at the house?

"Now, let's see," Mr. Cornwall said as he started shuffling through a few papers. He found one he liked, turned to the massive computer on his desk and started typing. He wrote something down on a small slip of paper and handed it to Trevor.

"Here is the balance on the account."

Trevor took the slip of paper and looked at it.

The account held $3,000,000.

Chapter Two

Within seconds, Trevor Campbell had become a millionaire. Three million dollars was a lot of money by 2003 standards; god knows what it worth in 1978. Twice as much? Three times as much? It didn't matter. It might even be worth being thrown back in time if it meant Trevor could be a millionaire. Earlier, while he was in the grocery store, he briefly worried that if he were stuck here for any length of time, he would have to start looking for a job. Now that wasn't necessary. He had just come into instant-retirement money.

Mr. Cornwall had had Trevor fill out some generic bank paperwork, and given him some temporary checks as well as some literature regarding potential investments Trevor could make with the money. As of right now, the money was all in cash, just sitting in a checking account. From what Trevor could tell, there was no catch to the money. It was a personal checking account solely in his name that he could access at any time, and, if he wanted to, he could withdraw the full $3,000,000 in cold hard cash.

What was more concerning, however, was what happened next. Mr. Cornwall informed Trevor that Ike Wallbauer had set up a safety deposit box in his name, and asked him if he wanted to see it. He said yes, and Mr. Cromwell took him to a back room. Trevor suddenly remembered the small key on the key ring, and pulled it out. Sure enough, it fit the lock on the safety deposit box Mr. Cromwell brought out to him.

Mr. Cromwell left Trevor alone in the small back room, and Trevor opened the steel box. The first thing that caught his eye was a pearl-handled, semi-automatic handgun and a box of 50 bullets. Next to the gun was a large brown envelope. The box was otherwise empty. Not wanting to leave his fingerprints on any mystery guns, Trevor avoided it and reached instead for the envelope. Inside was a birth certificate, Social Security card, some military discharge paperwork, and various other documents and pieces of paperwork chronicling his personal history.

All of it was forged. Every last bit of it would convince anyone that Trevor Campbell was born in 1940 and was now living in 1978. Today had been the craziest day of his life, so finding even more forged documents barely registered on his radar anymore. The gun was another story. Why did this Ike Wallbauer, his "associate," feel the need to leave him a weapon?

He decided to leave everything in the box for now. He might have to come back later and do something with the gun – bury it in the backyard or throw it in a river or something. Despite being in the Army, Trevor wasn't a big "gun nut," and he certainly didn't like his name being connected to any suspicious firearms. That's how people get framed for murder, if movies and TV were to be believed.

Trevor headed back home and ate lunch while looking over all of the financial information he had gotten from the bank. He should probably invest a good chunk of the money right off the bat; the 1980s were coming up, and Trevor knew that people made a ton of money in the stock market in the '80s. He needed to get on board with that, ASAP.

Trevor wondered if Ike Wallbauer was the mystery man who had left him notes around the house. Was he "from the future," too, or was he a "local?" Would he come back to see how everything was going, or was his job done? Trevor hoped *somebody* would be checking in on him, because he had no idea what was going on or what he was supposed to be doing.

For the rest of the day, Trevor stayed home, read the newspapers and magazines he bought at the store, and formulated a plan. Tomorrow he would make another run down to the shopping district to pick up more supplies and do a little more recon of the area. He would swing back by the bank, retrieve the gun, and ask Mr. Cromwell about investing some of his money. Then he would just lay low.

Trevor figured the best course of action would be to simply wait and see how things unfolded. He had been given no guidance on anything, so obviously somebody *had* to be getting in touch with him soon. Right? Trevor suddenly worried what would happen if this Ike Wallbauer (or whoever his "contact" was) died of a heart attack or a car accident before getting in touch with him, and he was just left stranded here in the late 1970's.

Around 7 o'clock in the evening, Trevor became extremely tired. He was nodding off on the couch watching the evening news, having just eaten a sandwich and some chips for dinner. He barely had the strength to drag himself to the bathroom, brush his teeth, pee, and peel his clothes off before falling into bed and passing out.

When Trevor woke up the next morning, he looked at his watch and was surprised to see it was almost 10 a.m. He had slept solidly for almost 15 hours. *I guess time* travel takes a lot out of a person, he thought. He got up, showered, dressed, and went to the kitchen to fix breakfast. After eating, he watched TV for a little bit before heading out to do some more shopping.

About a block down from the grocery store was a department store. These were still around in 2003, but their heyday had long since passed. The late '70s, on the other hand, was peak department store glory days. If the grocery store amazed him, the department store absolutely blew his mind. He vaguely remembered going into them when he was a small child, but their details didn't really register. Now it was like going into one of those big box stores from *his* time, but just… better. In every conceivable way.

Everything was just nicer, cleaner, bigger, better, and, like the grocery store, felt like walking into a pop culture museum. Even the people walking around, with their 1970's haircuts and clothes, added a whole other layer to the experience. It would be like if you visited the Louvre and all the other guests were wearing Renaissance garb or something. And you were able to buy the paintings for pennies on the dollar. With millions of dollars someone else had given you.

It was almost too much for Trevor to handle, but he had to stick to his plan. He wanted to buy a few more sets of clothes, including a suit. He also needed some kitchen appliances like a toaster, microwave, some pots and pans, and a coffee maker. In the electronics section, he got a telephone, two small radios, and the latest video game console which had just been released several months earlier. There were only eight or nine games available for it, but Trevor bought them all.

Around this time, his cart piled high, a store employee asked him if he would be interested in their home delivery service. Trevor excitedly took advantage of this, and grabbed another shopping cart to fill. He loaded up a basic 110-pound weight set, a small workout bench, and a door-mounted pull-up bar. "New Trevor" had obviously kept himself in shape, so "78 Trevor" figured he should continue the trend.

These were names he came up with for himself earlier in the day, just so he could keep his own timeline straight in his head. "Old Trevor" was the Trevor Campbell who existed from his birth up to the year 2003, when he turned 26. "New Trevor" was the Trevor Campbell that existed from the age of 26 to when he went back in time, somehow, at the age of, presumably, 37. "78 Trevor" was the Trevor Campbell that existed from when he woke up in that house in Minnesota on a cold January morning in 1978 up until now.

He decided to go back to the electronics section and get a record player, some speakers, and some records. He swung through the toy section and snagged a few toys just for the hell of it. He believed most men were still kids at heart, and he knew these would be worth a lot of money someday. There was a decent book selection as well, so he also stocked up on some reading material; fiction, non-fiction, and some more magazines.

In the outdoor section, Trevor picked up a shovel and few more basic tools. After grabbing some other random household goods and office supplies, Trevor decided this was enough shopping for one day. He paid for everything in cash, and the clerk told him the store truck would be by his house later that evening to drop everything off.

After leaving the department store, Trevor went back to the bank to talk to Mr. Cornwall about investing some of his riches. They hashed out a plan for his money, and Trevor went to his safety deposit box again to retrieve the gun and bullets. He felt like "celebrating" for some reason, so after leaving the bank, he stopped at a liquor store, stocked up on necessities, then hit a fast food restaurant to take some burgers and fries home.

Trevor ate his dinner while watching TV. Shortly after downing his third beer, the department store delivery truck showed up to drop off his goods. Trevor spent the remainder of the evening playing video games and drinking beer before going to bed shortly before midnight.

The next day was spent unpacking everything from the department store and setting up his house. Trevor turned the empty bedroom into his gym, and set up the workout equipment in there along with one of the radios.

He put the other radio in his bedroom and did a load of laundry to wash his new clothes. All of the kitchen equipment found a home, and the tools were put out in the garage on the shelving units. Trevor triple-wrapped the gun and bullets in some freezer bags, covered it with duct tape, then threw it in another freezer bag before burying it in the backyard. Once the grass grew back in the Spring, nobody would know anything was buried there. He made sure to only handle the gun with his gloves on after wiping it down with alcohol.

Trevor had been in 1978 for less than three days, but he already felt settled. He had always been quick to adjust to change, and could usually find contentment wherever life led him. He had enough money to last the rest of his life, and he was breaking in his home quite nicely, if he did say so himself. As he sat on the couch, relaxing after a workout and listening to some records, he started thinking of a long-term plan.

If nobody ever contacted him again, and he was left alone to fend for himself, he would spend the remainder of the year here in this house, just getting acclimated to living in the late 1970s. Then, early next year, he would start shopping around for a nicer, bigger house, probably somewhere warmer like the Southwest. Or maybe California.

Or what about Europe? He could afford to live very comfortably almost anywhere in the world now. No, Europe was too soon… that might be in the ten-year plan. He should definitely stay Stateside for awhile until he was sure he would never be able to solve the mystery of how he had gotten here.

If someone *did* ever contact him, and explained to him what was going on, well, he would just have to deal with it then, and hope he wouldn't have to pay back any of the money he had spent. According to Mr. Cromwell, however, and all of the paperwork from the bank, it seemed that all the money in his account was his, free and clear.

At least, *legally*, it was. Trevor seemed to have 12 years of his life unaccounted for, 12 years in which he had become a physically fit, shaggy-haired, time traveler. Who knows what he had gotten mixed up in during those 12 years? He could be a mafia hit man, for all he knew. That would certainly explain the gun and money.

What if he had been sent back in time to kill Jimmy Carter, or Henry Kissinger, or some politician he had never heard of? And why Minnesota? Was there some crucial event or person that brought him to this specific place, and this specific time? Trevor had read several newspapers by now, but nothing jumped out to him about Minnesota in January 1978 as having any sort of cosmic space-time significance.

No, he couldn't go too far off on these tangents. He had to work with what knew, and operate on facts and what he could see and hear. The pistol that was now buried three feet underground in his backyard was not an assassin's weapon. It was too loud and messy. It was a .45 caliber; a soldier's pistol, designed for war, built for stopping power. Ike Wallbauer had probably just left it for him for protection. He was a millionaire now, after all. Rich people had enemies just for being rich.

Trevor decided that the next day he would find a library and start doing some research. He had very little information to go on, but at least he had a name that he hoped wasn't an alias.

Chapter Three

Trevor stopped at the local gas station and was told there was a library about a mile down the road. Along the way, he spotted some other businesses that might prove useful; a post office, car mechanic, another grocery store, and a home improvement store.

The library was in a large, tan, brick building that looked very ugly to Trevor's eyes. It was probably the height of chic architecture in 1978, though. He parked his car, walked inside, and asked the librarian where all the phone books were. She led him to a long metal shelf full of dozens of phone books. Some from every state, covering every major metropolitan area in the country, and the entirety of Minnesota.

Trevor spent the next few hours poring through them, starting with the ones in Minnesota, and then working outwards to adjacent states. He could find no listing for anyone named Ike Wallbauer. Unless this Ike person traveled from several states over, his name was probably an alias. He decided to pause the phone book search for today and asked the librarian to help him find some science books. He needed to learn as much as he could about theoretical physics and time travel.

Trevor skimmed through several books, but wasn't able to learn much. The physics either went way over his head, or it was so vague and non-committal that it basically just boiled down to "eh, who knows." One thing he found very interesting was that, theoretically speaking, there was nothing in the known laws of physics that said time travel was technically impossible. It was simply a matter of figuring out how to do it. If Trevor Campbell's presence in 1978 was any indication, humans had indeed figured out how to do it sometime after 2003.

Trevor left the library and swung by the post office to grab some local phone books and buy some stamps. When he got home, he had an idea, so he flipped through one of the phone books and located a private detective. Since today was Saturday, he figured he should just relax the rest of the weekend and call the private detective on in a few days after getting a phone line hooked up. The phone books also had some extensive street maps of the city, which seemed like they would be immensely helpful.

Trevor spent the remainder of the weekend relaxing, watching TV, playing video games, and working out. Neither Ike

Wallbauer nor anyone else showed up to the house. On Monday, Trevor was able to set up a telephone line and called a private detective named Burt Harvard, who had an office less than three miles from Trevor's house. Harvard told Trevor he could come by his office that day if he was able to. Trevor said he was and got directions to Harvard's office.

Burt Harvard's office was in a small office complex housing a dentist, a lawyer, and an accountant. Trevor made a mental note of these businesses being here since they all sounded useful. Harvard's office was of course the smallest, and basically consisted of two rooms; the main office, and a room filled with file cabinets. Harvard was in his 50's and overweight, but had a shockingly thick head of gray hair. He was wearing an ill-fitting tan suit when he met Trevor at the front door.

"Mr. Campbell, come in. Nice to meet you," the two shook hands.

"Hello, Mr. Harvard."

"Please, call me Burt."

"Okay. I'm Trevor."

"So, Trevor, what can I do for you?" Burt asked as he sat behind his desk. Trevor sat opposite him in a rickety wooden chair and pulled a piece of paper out of the new sport coat he was wearing.

145

"I'd like to see if you can find a man named Ike Wallbauer. I have heard from third parties that he claims to know me, but I don't know him. He was possibly living in or renting the house in which I am currently staying. I believe this is a sample of his handwriting."

Trevor handed Burt the note from the kitchen taped to the box of toaster pastries. Trevor didn't want to tell him about the business card, the bank account being set up for him, and certainly not the gun. He figured that would lead to questions he couldn't answer. Burt studied the note.

"Do you mind if I make a copy of this?"

"Not at all."

Burt stood up and walked into his file room. Trevor looked around at the pictures and décor of Burt's office as he heard some sort of copy machine firing up. Burt Harvard was a Korean War veteran, and had apparently been a cop at some point. There were also a few pictures of him playing tennis. Several small trophies stood on a bookshelf, but Trevor couldn't see what they were for. Burt returned and handed Trevor the note.

"Anything else you can tell me about this Ike Wallbauer? Who are these third parties you spoke of?"

Trevor hesitated. He wanted to avoid talking about the bank.

"I would like to protect their identities if at all possible."

Burt slowly nodded, and said, "Okay. I'll just have to work with what you give me."

"One more thing," Trevor added. "I do know that Mr. Wallbauer may either be very wealthy, or at least connected to some very wealthy individuals."

Burt's eyes narrowed, and he jotted down this information on a notebook.

"Well, Trevor, I can at least do some basic record searches. This doesn't seem like a very common name, so if he's out there, I'll find him."

Trevor headed home after leaving Burt Harvard's office. That week, Trevor mostly stayed home. He thought about going out to a bar or restaurant or something, but he was still worried about casual conversation and having to explain his past and what he was doing with his life.

He went to the bank to retrieve all of the documents in his safety deposit box, and he studied them in an effort to piece together a new life for himself. His forged military history was thankfully quite mundane. Four years of service with no deployments and no valorous medals or actions. Nobody would be pushing him too hard on this or think it was suspicious.

The forged college degree was from the college that Trevor actually graduated from, and even in the same concentration. All of the other paperwork and legal documents matched Old Trevor's life as much as possible. Usually only the dates had been changed. Where things were not able to line up, the details of 78 Trevor's life were made simple and unimpressive. It certainly seemed that 78 Trevor's mission was to blend in to the background and not be anybody important. The millions of dollars in his bank account assured he would never need to jeopardize anything by having to look for a job or rely on too many connections.

So... what was he supposed to do? Just hang out for the rest of his life, playing video games and watching TV? Trevor formulated a theory. When he had traveled back in time, New Trevor's memory had somehow been erased. He was missing 12 years of his life, so it was entirely possible that the missing time contained the information that explained how and why he ended up in 1978. The only person that could even conceivably help him was Ike Wallbauer.

Over the next couple of months, Trevor settled into a routine. He would wake up and work out for about 30-40 minutes. His daily routine consisted of 100-200 push-ups, 30-50 pull-ups, and various leg exercises with the adjustable barbell; jump squats, calf raises, deadlifts, and maybe some abdominal work. Every other day he would do additional exercises like shoulder presses and barbell curls. He listened to music on the radio while he worked out.

After his workout, he would take a shower and then eat breakfast while reading the local and national newspapers he was now subscribed to, usually while listening to music on the radio or record player. If there were any chores to be done around the house, like laundry, dishes, sweeping, or shoveling snow, he would do this until lunchtime.

He would eat lunch while watching TV, usually game shows or sometimes the news. After lunch he would go for a long walk, sometimes around the neighborhoods, but sometimes up to the shopping district where he would just window shop, or maybe buy a book or new video game.

After returning home from his walk, Trevor would read for a while until dinner. He ate in the living room, watching TV for a couple of hours, and then read some more until bedtime. This couple of months was very relaxing for Trevor, and he felt like he was getting used to living in 1978.

Then, in mid-March, he got a call from Burt Harvard. Ike Wallbauer had been found. Every week or two Burt had called Trevor with an update, but usually no new information had been discovered. Now, however, there was good news. Burt had exhausted his resources for finding Ike in the United States, but by sheer happenstance an old cop buddy of his had moved to Canada and gotten a job with the RCMP. Some strings were pulled, and the Wallbauer family had been located in British Columbia.

Ted and Annette Wallbauer owned a stereo repair shop in Vancouver. They had one son, and his name was Ike. Ike Wallbauer was twelve years old in 1978. If this was the same Ike Wallbauer involved in Trevor's time travel escapades, then that meant that *he* was somehow traveling around in time as well, because there's no way a 12-year-old could have set all this up for Trevor.

Burt had said the Wallbauer stereo repair shop was doing quite well, and the owners were thinking of opening up two more locations. The Wallbauers weren't exactly living high on the hog, but if their business did well over the years, by the time Ike grew up and inherited their wealth or the company, he

150

may well be a millionaire. He could then travel back in time with his riches and set things up for Trevor. Burt said this was the only Ike Wallbauer he could find in North America. He had even checked several countries in Europe where he had connections.

Pieces were starting to fall into place for Trevor, but it was ultimately a dead end. He couldn't go to a 12-year-old Ike in 1978 and ask him why his future self became a time traveler. But now he had a crucial piece of information. There was a strong chance that the Ike Wallbauer helping Trevor had traveled from the future as well, and was not a 1978 local. There were now two people, most likely, that had traveled back in time – Trevor Campbell and Ike Wallbauer. If two could do it, why not three? Or ten? Were there more time travelers out there that Trevor could get help from?

And the fact that Burt could not find an adult Ike Wallbauer anywhere in North America *right now* strongly suggested that Ike had left 1978 and traveled back to the future... which meant there was a chance Trevor could travel back home as well.

The rest of 1978 was fairly uneventful. Burt checked in every month to report on the Wallbauer's repair business, which continued to do well. Trevor got a part-time job as a dishwasher at a local bar, just for something to do. He obviously didn't need the money, but decided it might be a good idea to "get out in the world" and try to live normally for a while. He still planned on moving next year to a nicer house in another state if nobody from the future ever came to get him.

Trevor even dated a few women that he met through the bar. He never let on that he was a millionaire, instead explaining that he made his income from the dishwashing job and a side gig he had as a technical writer. This of course was a lie, but it was an easy lie to live with since it didn't involve him having to go anywhere or really prove anything. When pressed, he simply said that he wrote boring, generic manuals for electronics companies to use for internal training. He even bought a word processor and set it up in his dining room to complete the illusion.

Of course, Trevor was never very suave with women, so those relationships usually didn't last long. He hadn't really made any other friends, but Burt started inviting him to cookouts and barbecues he hosted on various holidays. Trevor was paying him a decent amount every month to do nothing more than a half-hour's worth of work getting updates on the Wallbauer family, so Burt felt he at least owed him some spare ribs.

By the end of 1978, Trevor was basically resigned to the fact he was now stuck in the past. No one had ever contacted him, and nothing remotely suspicious ever happened to make him think he was being followed or watched. In January, 1979, Trevor contacted a real estate agent and begun talks of selling the house. Some of the paperwork in the safety deposit box related to the house, which turned out to be completely in Trevor's name.

Then, on January 31st, 1979, Trevor received a letter in the mail from Ike Wallbauer.

Chapter Four

There was no return address on the letter, and the handwriting matched that of the bank business card and kitchen note that Trevor still held on to and had tacked up on his refrigerator. It was a short letter, and read:

"Dear Trevor,

Hope you are doing well. Saw you at the bar but I didn't want to interfere. The boys up on the Hill would have my hide if they knew I was even writing you this letter, but I just had to apologize. I'm sorry I sent you back with your history of head trauma. I didn't think it would be an issue but I guess I was wrong. I know that's why you haven't been making the drops, and I also know about Burt Harvard. I just hope you haven't lost too much of your memory, and you're still the Trevor Campbell I respect and admire. And I'm sorry I can't bring you back. There are just too many risks now. Well, gotta go. Enjoy the money!

Regards,
Ike

155

That was it. Trevor stood in his living room and read the letter over and over, probably a good 20 times. So, his theories turned out to be correct. Ike Wallbauer was the one who had sent him back in time. His head injury in Iraq in 2003 caused his memory loss when he made the trip to 1978. And he was officially stuck in the past now. The letter raised some more questions, though.

Ike mentioned some "drops" that Trevor had not been making. Obviously, he was supposed to be carrying out some sort of mission, and had failed to do so. Also, Ike had found out about Burt, and had even spied on Trevor on at least one occasion. Was he still here, now, in 1979? Or did he just "pop back" in time to mail a letter? It didn't matter, because it sounded like he would never be contacting Trevor again.

Trevor sold the house in Minnesota, and moved to a much nicer one in the north of New Mexico. The years rolled by, and Trevor enjoyed being old enough to appreciate the 1980's the second time around. By the end of the decade, he had grown very wealthy, and he moved to Los Angeles.

Trevor began dating a woman who was a film producer, and after several years they ended up getting married. By the year 2000, through investing in certain key

156

computer and technology stocks over many years, along with a side gig of movie producing, Trevor's net worth was in the hundreds of millions of dollars. He lived a life of luxury, but also donated large portions of his income to numerous charities.

Trevor never told his wife that he was a time traveler. By the time they met, he had already invested over a dozen years living in the past, so it wasn't hard to keep it a secret. Trevor actually sat down in the early '80's and, over the course of a week, wrote himself a basic fake autobiography so he could keep the fictitious events and details of his life straight. It was over 30 pages long, and he would skim through it every once in a while to make sure he could keep his story straight.

September 11, 2001 was coming up, and Trevor wondered if he should warn some friends of his living in New York City that they should get out of town. He invited them to come vacation for a few days, but they couldn't make it. After the attacks, he thankfully discovered that they had survived.

In 2003, on the date that he would be injured in Iraq, Old Trevor was 26 years old, and 78 Trevor was 63 years old. He sat in his study in Beverly Hills, sipping cognac, and wondered what would happen now. His knowledge of the future ended as of today.

He had been ahead of the game for 25 years, but now that was over. Years earlier, Trevor decided against ever contacting another version of himself, in fear it might disrupt the space-time continuum or something. He later learned that Specialist Bradley unfortunately did not survive the IED blast, but Staff Sergeant Moss had. Within days of hearing the news, Trevor donated $1,000,000 to a wounded veterans charity.

He was, however, seriously contemplating getting in touch with Ike Wallbauer. Trevor had kept Burt Harvard on the payroll for years until the P.I.'s death in 1993. Every month Burt would call and report on the Wallbauers. Their repair business expanded to selling all kinds of electronics, and they flourished and became millionaires. Ike grew up and took control of the family's operations in Seattle.

After Burt died, Trevor decided not to concern himself anymore with the Wallbauers. Things were obviously headed in the right direction and he didn't want to get too involved and start risking things. Then, in 2008, Trevor decided to check in on Ike. In the late '90s he left the family business, gone to college, and gotten a math degree. He turned out to be a prodigy, got a Masters in physics, and then a PhD. He was then hired by a military contracting company, and, Trevor assumed, began working on time travel experiments. According to his calculations, Trevor figured he was sent back in time sometime around the year 2015.

Trevor turned 75 years old in 2015. He was still in great health, and he wondered if that was due to a lifetime of exercise and mostly clean eating, or if the military had injected him with some kind of super serum before sending him back in time, in order to give him the best chance of survival. By the end of 2016, Trevor was 76 years old and almost a billionaire. He decided to write Ike Wallbauer a short letter, in care of the defense contractor's address.

"Dear Ike,

Thank you for everything. My life has turned out great. Let me know if you ever need anything.

Regards,
Trevor"

Two weeks later, the letter was returned to him, unopened. Across the front of the envelope, a single word had been stamped in blocky red letters – DECEASED.

Trevor didn't know how to feel. He searched for Ike on the internet every once in a while, just to keep tabs, but he kept a very low profile. Then, after his letter was returned, Trevor spent hours online searching for any details he could find. He eventually located a press release from the defense contractor, dated in early 2016, regarding an accident. It read:

"Early this morning, a mechanical failure in some experimental equipment resulted in the death of a scientist and two soldiers from the Special Forces Operational Detachment – Delta. Names are currently being withheld for reasons of national security."

That was it. No follow up, no news articles, no obituaries, no more press releases. Was Trevor one of the Delta Force Operators that had supposedly died in an experimental time machine? Was Ike Wallbauer really dead, or was he hiding out, somewhere in time?

Trevor tried to make sense of it all. Sometime after 2003, he must have recovered from his injuries and eventually joined Delta Force. Meanwhile, the military had Ike working on time travel experiments, and he needed warm bodies to test it on. The military either asked for volunteers from Delta Force, or just plain whored-out Trevor, to take part in the experiments.

Two Delta Force Operators and Ike Wallbauer had supposedly been killed in a time machine accident. But Trevor had survived, and so had Ike, at least for a little while. The military was apparently using their deaths as cover for the success of the time travel experiments. It made perfect sense; obviously the government didn't want the general public to know that time travel was possible. It could literally alter the course of humanity, from pre-history to the distant future. Whoever controlled time travel would rule the world forever.

Trevor could never figure out why he had been sent back in time to the year 1978, specifically. Ike Wallbauer had no connection to the area. Nothing significant happened there in the late 1970's, or even since then. But perhaps that's why Minnesota in 1978 was chosen; a completely non-descript time and place, for history's first time travelers to dip their toe in the stream of time.

Trevor was supposed to be making "drops," but failed to do that after losing his memory. What sort of information was he supposed to have been reporting on? Basic day-to-day living in the past? Or was he supposed to be assassinating someone after all?

And then there was the matter of the second Delta Force Operator involved in the experiments. If Trevor was still alive, there's a good chance the second Operator was, too. But who was he? Where was he? *When* was he? Was his memory intact?

These were all questions for which he would never have an answer. Not unless Ike Wallbauer showed up again. Trevor would not be surprised if he was laying on his death bed in 20 years and a 50-something Ike showed up to bring him flowers.

Several months later, Trevor received a package in the mail with no return address. He opened it to see a folded piece of paper sitting on a mass of foam packing peanuts. He unfolded the paper and read it:

"Trevor,

Hey, dude… long time no see. Thought you might want this stuff as a little souvenir. Good to see you're enjoying life!

Deke"

Deke? Who was Deke? Trevor reached his hand into the foam peanuts, and removed the "souvenir." It was a wooden cigar box, with something heavy shifting around inside of it. Trevor cautiously opened the lid of the cigar box, and exposed the front page of a folded-up newspaper. It was folded in such a way that Trevor could see it was a newspaper from Minnesota, dated two days *after* he had moved to New Mexico in 1979.

Trevor lifted up the newspaper to see what else was in the box. His heart skipped a beat once he saw the pearl-handled pistol he had buried in his snowy Minnesota backyard, almost 40 years earlier.